The Stolen Seasons

The Stolen Seasons
By DAVID DIVINE

THOMAS Y. CROWELL COMPANY • NEW YORK

Drawing and map by CHARLES ROBINSON

First published in the United States of America in 1970
Copyright © 1967 by DAVID DIVINE

Designed by CAROLE FERN HALPERT

Manufactured in the United States of America

L.C. Card 77–127604

ISBN 0–690–77458–3

1 2 3 4 5 6 7 8 9 10

To
Ewen James MacAlister Campbell

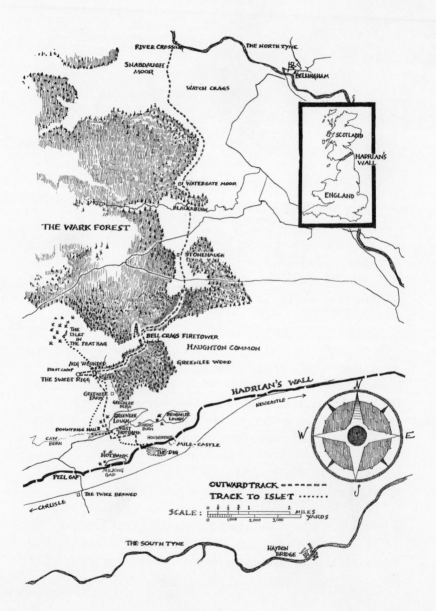

1

"We can't use the bridge," said Peter reasonably. "There wasn't a bridge in Roman times."

"Then," said his father, shifting his hat over his eyes, "you will get excessively wet, you will all three of you catch preposterous colds, you will return sneezing, and your mother will take it out on me."

Mig said, without any tone in her voice at all, "Mother will be so glad to see us back in one piece that you'll get away with it. She always is, and you always do."

Mr. Manson lifted one side of his hat and looked malevolently at his daughter, but when he spoke again it was to the American boy who lay on the other side. "Clint, do you treat your father with such phe*nom*enal irreverence?"

"No, *sir!*" answered Clinton hurriedly.

"Huh!" Mig managed to convey scorn, reproach, and disbelief in equal proportions in a single syllable.

"None the less"—Manson's voice was equable—"there *is* a bridge just round the corner beyond Tarset Castle."

"We'll use it if we have to," said Peter. "I promise. But the water's low, Dad. I'll work out a crossing myself first . . ."

"On the principle," interjected his father lazily, "that it's better to drown one than drown three. Something in that! At least you can swim, and the North Tyne isn't the Amazon. All right, use your head! You can swim, Clint?"

The American boy removed the straw that he was chewing from his mouth. "I can swim," he affirmed; "since I was six, I guess."

Mr. Manson sat up and pushed his hat to the back of his head. "Let's go over the ground rules. You have to reach Hadrian's Wall without being seen. If anybody *does* see you, pull back as if you were dodging a Roman patrol and start again from dead ground. You must stick to the agreed times crossing the Wall, and you mustn't be spotted. Right?" He looked at them questioningly. "Let battle commence." He climbed to his feet and stared down at them. "Back to civilization Wednesday evening. You phone us not later than eight o'clock, and I don't care if it means walking ten miles to a telephone—not later than eight. Clear?"

"Not later than eight," said Peter solemnly.

"Mig?"

"Not later than eight."

"Make a note of it, Clint!" Manson stood looking down at the boy. "I don't want this to develop into an international incident."

"No, *sir*." Clinton wasn't quite certain how to fit into what was clearly a traditional family situation.

Mig got up in one quick movement, lifted her rucksack, and slipped the straps of the frame over her shoulders. The others followed suit. Manson watched them sardonically. When they had settled their loads, they looked at him.

"Matches?" he asked with sarcastic eyebrows. "Can opener? Bottle opener? Adhesive tape? Clean socks? Aspirin? The *Financial Times*?"

"When you've quite finished," said his daughter with mock respect, "we'll start."

Manson raised his hand in salute. "Start!" And as they turned away, he shouted in a tremendous voice, "Tarret Burn and Tarset Burn. Yet! Yet! Yet!"

Clinton looked round startled, but Manson's children walked on unflinching—they were used to their father.

Only Mig muttered, "Where did he find that?"

Peter answered her softly over his shoulder, "I think it was the battle cry of the Moss Troopers from the burns. He probably sat up half the night searching for it."

"Yet! Yet! Yet!" The American boy repeated the words. "It's got something."

"It must have had in the old days. They were a thieving lot—right up into Scotland, right down to Durham. Yet! Yet! Yet!" Peter savored the words. "Do us for a battle cry perhaps."

"We could do worse," said Mig approvingly.

They quickened their pace, striding down the slope of the stubble towards the blue water of the river.

Down the slope after them came their father's voice again. "If you light any fires on Forestry Commission land, they'll hang you from a fir tree."

"He knows we wouldn't!" said Mig indignantly.

But Peter only raised a hand in acknowledgment without turning round. "He knows, but he feels that a reminder now and again helps."

The girl laughed suddenly and surprisingly, remembering earlier misdeeds.

After a little, Manson turned back towards the road. When he wheeled round again as he reached the car, there was no sign of them. He peered into the glove compartment, looked at the floor at the back and at the ledge below the rear window. "Mig's actually forgotten nothing," he muttered

to himself, "at least in the car. I'd call that a good start."
He turned the ignition key.

They took off their packs in a minute shelter between a
thorn bush and a hazel thicket.

Peter said, "We've got to do this thing properly. If the
Romans had patrols out, they'd be watching the regular
fords, but they'd never have men enough to watch the
whole river. We're fourteen miles north of the Wall here
as the crow flies—more than a day's march out and home
even for auxiliaries, and a longer distance the way the
cavalry would have to come. I don't think we have to bother
about a regular watch. The biggest danger would be from
a patrol on the move, and a patrol would keep well above
the river meadows. I think we'll get by."

"How are you going to cross it?" asked Mig.

"Stick. Sounding stick. We'll get a straight one off the
hazels. Cut it for me while I try the shallows." Peter rolled
up his shorts and began to take off his boots and stockings.

Clinton opened a knife and approached the hazel. "How
long d'you want it?"

"About up to the level of my nose," replied Peter grimly.
"I don't breathe well after that."

Clinton laughed.

Mig said absently, "There's a reed warbler . . ."

"Skip the bird watching," snapped Peter, "and work out
how *you're* going to get across! You're four and three-
quarter inches shorter than I am." He slid down the bank,
looked cautiously up and down the river, and reported back
over his shoulder: "Not a member of the Bellinjum Anglers'
Club in sight. Two swans at about a hundred and eighty
yards, one moorhen, and something I can't see properly.
How's the stick going?"

"Just about," said Clinton. "You didn't want it strong
enough to take your weight, did you?"

"Just a sounding stick. I'd look silly sitting on it."

"Okay." The other boy handed down a neatly peeled hazel wand. "Show better in the peat water—and I reckon it's peat water."

"Looks like whisky," said Peter abstractedly, "but it's peat water all right. Here goes!"

He moved off cautiously, the water up to his knees. A moment later it was halfway up his thighs. It stayed there for a time; then they saw the sounding stick go suddenly deep. Peter stood prodding for a little before they heard him say softly, "No go." Alternately prodding and lifting the stick, he moved downstream almost forty yards, and after a moment, apparently satisfied, moved forward again. The bottom shelved suddenly, and they could see his knees —there was evidently a mid-stream ridge—then gradually it deepened again. He carried on until it all but lapped the rolled-up edge of his shorts. Again he worked downstream, prodding.

"Think he can do it?" Clinton asked.

"Sure-*ly*!" Mig had borrowed the expression from the boy. "May take a bit of time, but he's patient." She watched the diminishing figure of her brother lazily.

Peter was stock-still in the middle of the river now. He was staring down into the water, looking a bit like a heron fishing. He stood like this for perhaps a minute; then suddenly he went straight ahead—the water halfway up his thighs—reached the opposite bank, and disappeared into a little thicket.

After three minutes he reappeared, this time carrying two sticks. Carefully satisfying himself that everything was clear, he strode confidently into the stream. When he reached the point that he was looking for he stopped, lunged down with a sounding stick, and walked on, leaving the stick behind him bending with the current. Again he moved confidently.

Mig said, "He's marking the downstream end of the deep patches, I bet."

"How can he be certain?" demanded Clinton.

"Counted his steps."

They watched as the boy paused again, plunged in the second stick, and waded on boldly.

"How would you have crossed a river like this in the States?"

Clinton plucked the straw that he was chewing from between his teeth. "Six-lane highway," he said laconically.

Mig squinted at him. "No, I mean if you were on a raid like this."

"No Roman walls. Embassy kids don't get to playing around the backwoods much anyways."

"City slicker!" retorted the girl derisively.

Peter reached the bank. He had an air of importance as of one who has achieved great things. "I've marked the safe route," he announced.

Mig looked at him fondly. "If you'd let us bring swimsuits, you wouldn't have needed to. I bet we could go straight across with our packs on our heads."

"Girls!" said Peter distantly.

They stood up and began to get their packs together.

"I'm still four and three-quarter inches shorter than you. What do I do?" Mig asked.

"Get wet!" replied her brother callously. "We take our shorts off and go over in our pants. You've got a dry pair. I know—I heard Mother tell you for the third time."

They made the necessary adjustments, and Peter walked into the shallows again.

Over his shoulder he said, "I don't think we need to use a line unless you want to, Mig."

"I'll survive," answered Mig tolerantly.

The markers were clear enough from the start, their

white peeled stubs moving easily with the tug of the water. None the less the difference of four and three-quarter inches was too much—Mig was wet to the waist long before they reached the first.

As they passed, Peter said to Clinton in the rear, "Pull it up and leave it to float. No sense in leaving anything to show where we've passed."

They changed direction to the second marker. Thoughtfully Mig tucked her shirt up even higher. They passed it, and it too was left to drift downstream. Two minutes later they were on the south bank ensconced in the farther thicket.

Peter pushed his way straight through to the edge of it, and at once they heard him say, "Dam!"

"Tinker's dam!" Mig supplemented the expletive. Clinton cocked an inquiring eye at her. "Dad lets us use it. He says if he didn't let us use something we'd prob'ly bust."

Her brother, coming back to the little clearing, said: "Prob'ly burst."

Mig snorted.

Clinton asked, "But why tinker's?"

"It was the little bit of clay that tinkers stuck under a place they were soldering to stop the solder running away."

"Oke. That'll come in useful. What were you griping about?"

"Enemy," said Peter shortly. "Enemy with a border collie just come into the top end of the field. We'll have to lie low. Better get our things on so that we can get away quickly if we have to."

Mig undid her pack and found her dry pants, went out of sight and changed.

Peter surveyed the seat of his own shorts ruefully. They were soaking wet, but he put them on perforce. When he had slipped on his boots he went back to the lookout place.

They heard him say, "Sitting on a stone, smoking a pipe, and talking to his dog. Hasn't he anything better to do?" He came back and sat down himself.

Clinton asked, "Where do we go from here?"

"There's a wall and a hedge about a hundred yards downstream. I planned to work down to that and go up to the road, using it as cover. But we can't if he's still there."

They sat silent, considering the fact.

Finally Mig said, "We could, of course, go up the other side of it."

Peter looked puzzled. "I didn't think of that," he admitted frankly.

Clinton chuckled. "And after?"

"Watch the road until we're certain there's nothing coming, get across it and into the pasture on the other side, and strike up over Snabdaugh Moor."

"How much?"

"Snabdaugh."

"Thought that was what you said. What does it mean?"

"I don't know."

"Crazy, man, crazy!" said Clinton derisively. "Mebbe if my pop does another tour of duty in London, I'll take time off and learn English."

Mig, lazily staring up into the blue of the sky, murmured, "Tallahassee and Yoakum and Kankakee. D'you want me to go on?"

The American boy hesitated. "Indians," he said with the air of one putting down a final card.

"Picts," said Mig with a gambler's throw.

Clinton threw up a hand in surrender. "And after this Snabdaugh?"

Peter thought for a moment. "We head for the Watch Crags. It's forest to the south of that. We'll turn southeast along the edge of the trees."

"Let's see the map."

"No map! We're tribesmen coming down from the Highlands, I keep telling you! We might have somebody who'd been this way before, and we'd have what we picked up from the friendly tribes, but we wouldn't have a map."

Mig said, "I don't see why not. They had rock maps up on Wheatwood Moor—and *that* was in early British times."

"Still doesn't allow us a one-inch Ordnance Survey map! We can't use it unless we get into trouble. We agreed that with Dad."

"Draw one then," said Clinton. "Draw one from what you remember and what you've been told. Seems sensible to me. A raiding party'd want something to go by if it lost its guide."

"You're not going to lose me!" retorted Peter.

"They'd do it on a sheepskin or something. We haven't got a sheepskin." Mig scrabbled in her rucksack. "Do it on a page of this." She handed over a bird-watching notebook. "And make it clear!"

Peter became absorbed. "We'll use the river as a base line. It runs like this." He made a sinuous line across the paper, descending a little towards the right-hand side. "The Tarset Burn comes in here"—he added a squiggle—"and this is Bellinjum. The road wasn't there then. Might have been a track though. We're here." He put a dot on the south bank of the river. "I reckon it's a mile and a half due south to the Watch Crags."

"Compass?" Clinton asked.

"No compass. They'd use the North star at night and the sun by day."

"And after the Watch Crags?"

"Forest. We keep clear of it."

"Real forest?"

"Forestry Commission forest," said Mig, "and that's real enough."

"We'll turn southeast along the edge of it till we reach

the corner here"—Peter drew in a long line to represent the edge of the Wark forest—"then it turns back here, and we turn with it. I reckon that's another mile and a half from the Watch Crags, and then there's a bit that juts out about here—I'd say another mile and a half to the southwest—narrow bit, if I remember properly. And I think the path went straight across it past a farm on the other side of the Blackaburn." He warmed up to his task. "We'll have to be careful getting past that. I don't think you can reckon on a friendly settlement anywhere between the North Tyne and the Wall. Stands to reason the patrols would watch them—they'd be scared." He thought for a moment. "Gets complicated after that. There's a highish hill and then the Wark Burn, and then there's a clear patch, I remember, that goes deep into the middle of the forest and a road that crosses it. There's a path through the next stretch of trees"— he was sketching vigorously now—"'bout two and a half miles down from Blackaburn. If we can find that, it'll save us a long way round. We come out at the top of Haughton Common; we ought to be able to see the Wall from there and we'll camp there or thereabouts. It's about twelve miles as we'll go. That'll leave us four miles for the morning—rough miles, but Mig's done more than that before."

Mig snorted indignantly. "I lasted better than you on Shap Fell!"

Clinton let his eyes flick mischievously from one to the other, wondering whether to encourage a brawl, but decided against it. "Mark the rivers—all right, burns then—so's I can get the lie of things."

Peter brought the North Tyne curling down from Bellingham with his pencil and drew a series of tributaries plunging off the moor to feed it. "We go over them at right angles till we pass the Wark Burn. After that we're on high ground."

"And then?"

"We slip across the Wall without being seen."

"When?"

"*Not* at dawn. Sentries are always on the lookout at dawn. Some time well after sunup when they're bored with looking and drowsy with the sun on their backs."

"And if we're seen?"

"Back to square one," said Mig flippantly.

"Back into dead ground," explained Peter, glowering at her, "and start all over again from a different angle." He got to his feet and went to the field edge. "Still sitting," they heard him say, "still smoking." He came back to the clearing.

"How'd you talk yourself into this?" asked Clinton softly.

Peter ignored the sarcasm. "The Prof's started a new dig a mile to the east of Milking Gap, and I said the Wall couldn't have been any good against infiltration, and he said, 'Why?' And I said any boy with a grapnel could have got across it in thirty seconds when the sentries' backs were turned. And he said, 'You get down to the new dig without being seen, and I'll put a note to that effect in the paper I'll write on it.' And . . . and here we are."

"Here we *all* are," said Clinton, "stuck on a river bank, held up by a pipe, a dog, and a man."

Mig abandoned her brother. "Talks too much—always talks too much. Come on! Let's get going and try the other side of the hedge. Yet! Yet! Yet!"

2

Manson walked up the slope of the close-cropped turf with an easy stride. One of Carrick's students was emptying a wheelbarrow of sieved soil on the spoil dump. Manson said, "Is the Professor about?"

The young man looked at him suspiciously. For a moment he hesitated, then he demanded, "Does he know you?"

"He does," said Manson shortly.

The student straightened himself. "Dr. Carrick!"

Carrick's body loomed up out of a shallow trench. He climbed clear of the rubble and said with a shadow of the same suspicion, "Now what the devil brought *you* here?"

"My young," answered Manson cheerfully. "You are about to be attacked. I saw them crossing the North Tyne just short of Tarset Castle about an hour ago. I reckon Mig was wet up to her navel. When I left they seemed to be held up by a farmer in a field."

"Fording it?" A gleam of humor replaced the suspicion in Carrick's eye.

"Fording it," agreed Manson solemnly. "No bridges, no roads, no maps, no fires, no human contacts. They should be pretty savage by the time they reach you."

"Tarset Castle . . ." Carrick made a quick calculation. "Some time tomorrow then. I didn't think . . ."

"If they're going to be a nuisance," said Manson bluntly, "shoo them away. They'll understand."

"Not a nuisance," Carrick answered hurriedly. "Peter's got something, you know. It's a point I hadn't thought of— I want his views. But"—he seemed to make his mind up with a rush— "we're on to something unexpected here."

Manson realized suddenly the extent of the atmosphere of suspicion—Carrick, after all, was an old friend. His voice was even more blunt as he said, "All right, I'll try to intercept them somewhere above Wark, but I can't guarantee that I'll be able to. Peter's making his own route."

Carrick raised a protesting hand. "No, no! I don't mean that at all. Look!" He came to a swift decision. "I can't tell you as a newspaperman yet, but I can as a friend. Come and look at this!" He led the way back to the trench.

Two young women were on all fours at the bottom of it, working away at the dry soil with brushes.

"I may be wrong, but there's a good chance that this is the biggest single find that's yet been made along the Wall. Miss Kirton, could you come up for a minute?"

Peering down into the trench, Manson saw a long curved edge of metal. Only a short segment of it was free on the face side. It appeared to have a regular pattern along its edge. The back was plain.

Carrick said, "We're not sure yet. It could be something pretty nearly as important as the great Mildenhall dish. Solid silver—look! Someone was using a trowel when it was located. Look at the scratch!"

Manson, down on his knees now, could see the gleam of silver. The rest of the curve was dark with oxidation. "Like the Mildenhall?" He whistled. "When . . .?"

"Yesterday afternoon about three o'clock. Everybody's sworn to secrecy. We've got to establish the stratification, and it's going to be the devil's own job. Look at the blocks of ashlar! They're absolutely interlocked round it, and we're going to have to work it all away before we can clear it and sort out the layers. It'll take days still."

"And you don't want a crowd hanging around?"

"We do *not!*" said Carrick fervently. "And more than that—you remember the dig at the ford below Raeburn Foot?"

"I remember hearing . . ."

"It wasn't one of mine," the Professor broke in hurriedly, "but Purvis told me that they got away with two statuettes and an arm purse and some coins. And there was that trouble at York last week. There's been at least one attempt on the museum at Chester too, and"—he made a loose gesture— "there are about five or six cases of finds disappearing, and always the good stuff. This . . ." He made a little upward movement of one hand.

"Have you told the police?"

"No." Carrick shook his head vaguely. "They wouldn't be interested. Why should they be? They'd say, 'Get it out and put it in a safe place.' "

"Why don't you?" asked Manson practically.

"The stratification, man, the stratification! This has an established provenance. It isn't like the Mildenhall dish— found four years before the professionals got on to it. You don't realize—one coin, one piece of pottery, that we could date accurately would establish everything that we need."

"Everything?"

"The date that this was wrecked over it, for instance . . ."

"And that would be important?"

"You know damn well it would be important!" retorted Carrick belligerently. "I thought . . ."

Manson grinned at his friend. "I know, I know! But I'm just trying to establish the facts as a newspaperman.

What was this place? You didn't tell me when you said that you were going to open it up."

"We hadn't an idea," confessed Carrick frankly. "We discovered it through those photographs that we took in the melting snow two years ago. There wasn't anything much that you could see on the surface. Just a few humps on the ground. But the photographs showed a building. I haven't made up my mind yet. It was a house, *not* a villa—just a small house but well built. Could be that of a commander of the garrison at Housesteads who wanted somewhere where he could get away from the garrison. It's got the air of a top person's cottage. We aren't deep enough yet. There are a lot of problems that have to be resolved. But it's interesting. And now this . . ." He paused for a moment as if trying to find the proper word and went on solemnly, "This is superb."

"Have you let Carew know?" Manson mentioned the name of the doyen of all the Wall's archaeologists.

"No, we've let nobody know yet except you, and you're an accident. I'll tell him as soon as I know something for certain—anything." He scratched the back of his head. "But I'll bet he'll arrive here by chance any moment now. He's got a nose for things."

Manson laughed. "I still think you ought to tell the police."

Carrick shook his head. "We left a volunteer on guard last night. We'll have somebody else tonight. Nobody knows this outside the twelve of us here—and you."

"I'm the thirteenth," said Manson warningly.

"You won't talk." Carrick brushed the possibility aside. "We're all right until the news gets out."

"Were they at the ford at Raeburn Foot?"

Carrick frowned. "That's a point." He called out, "Witton!"

A young man with an intellectual fringe of beard climbed up from a pit. He said in a rather high-pitched voice: "Doctor?"

"Come over here! You were at Raeburn Foot with Abercrombie, weren't you?"

"I was."

"What happened?"

"You mean with the dig, sir?"

"I don't mean with the dig. I mean with the statuettes."

"Of course. Sneak thieves, I think—just sneak thieves." Manson asked, "When did it happen?"

"Midday. We used to go down to the stream to eat our lunch. There was a pool there—pretty place."

"And?"

"And when we went back, they were gone," said Witton.

"You mean you just left them lying around?"

"Oh, no!" Witton bristled. "They were on a tray and they were properly marked and recorded."

"Still, you just left them there when you went to lunch."

"The place is in the middle of nowhere!" Witton's note of protest increased.

"I'm afraid we are careless on digs once the stuff is accounted for," said Carrick. "We never used to have this sort of thing."

"Is that all, sir?"

Manson said: "Just one more question. When were the statuettes discovered?"

"We'd only got them out that morning."

"No," said Manson quickly. "When did you first discover that they were there?"

"The previous day, I think," Witton replied, "—or it may have been the day before that. I know one head was clear. We knew what it was, of course. Why?"

"I was just thinking about opportunity," said Manson abstractedly.

3

"No gate." Peter sounded faintly aggrieved. There was a gate on the side that he had hoped to use.

Mig said, "We go over the wall then." She half turned to Clinton. "*And* you replace any stones that you knock down!"

"Why?" demanded Clinton promptly.

"Because in this country 'the rude uncouth shepherds of the borders' "—she was evidently quoting from somewhere—"rise up out of the ground and ask why you didn't—and they can be pretty uncouth doing it!" She turned to her brother. "Peter, have you ever seen a couth shepherd?"

"No such word," replied her brother humorlessly.

"Must be," said the girl. "You can't be 'un' if somebody else isn't *it*."

Clinton laughed softly. "I never had a sister."

"Some people have all the luck!" snapped Peter. Over his shoulder he asked, "What's he doing now?"

"Sittin' on a rock, smokin' his pipe, and talkin' to his dog," said the American boy swiftly. "He's got a considerable capacity for sittin'."

They heard the thud of Peter's pack as he dropped it

across the wall. "All clear!" he said. "I'm going over." He climbed cleverly, avoiding the long bramble shoots, changed foot at the top and dropped lightly to the roadside. "It's all right. He's looking the other way. Pack, Mig!"

The girl handed her pack across and was over the wall as neatly as her brother. Clinton's pack followed. He moved a little less certainly, unable to judge the solidity of the dry-stone wall, but he got over without accident—nothing fell.

"Quick!" urged Peter. "Get across before a car comes and look out for wire on the other side!"

They scurried across the road, dropped their packs beyond the next wall, and climbed hurriedly where Peter indicated. In a moment they had negotiated the single strand of wire and were in the field beyond the road. Instead of moving forward, Peter squatted in the shelter of the second wall. Methodically he began to scan the steep slope of the moor ahead of them.

"Flock of black-faced," he said at last.

"Black-faced what?"

"Sheep," Mig answered for Peter.

"You mean there'll be a sheepherder?" Clinton was beginning to jump at possibilities.

"Could be," said Peter, "but no reason at this time of year, not on a low slope like this. It's the sheep themselves."

"They scare easy," Mig explained.

"Easily," her brother corrected.

"Either way they'd give us away. What are you going to do?"

"Work round to the left," replied Peter confidently. "There's dead ground beyond. They won't see us. Do you see anything that looks like a human being, Clint?"

"Nary a thing."

"Right! On packs. Let's go!" He struck off to the left,

keeping to the edge of the pasture. They moved over a small rise. Beyond it in the hollow he saw a hedge. "We'll use that."

They worked their way to it and turned uphill. At once it was apparent that he had estimated his ground accurately. The shallow valley had a stream bed, dry in the September sun. The sheep were grazing beyond the western ridge. Ahead of them the valley was empty, running up from the cultivated ground beside the road to rough pasture and naked moor beyond.

They walked hard and in silence for a long time. Then Peter asked over his shoulder again, "What's he doing now?"

"Sittin' on a rock, smokin' his pipe, an' talkin' to his dog. Must have a powerful lot to say!"

All three laughed.

Fifty paces farther the shoulder of the moor hid them. Peter kept up the pace for another five minutes and then said, "Spell-o!" They slipped out of their packs and collapsed on the turf, laughing again for no particular reason.

"I reckon we've made it. Nobody saw us cross the river, and we saw nobody. He"—Peter jerked his thumb in the general direction of the farmer in the field—"didn't spot us . . ."

"His dog did," Clinton broke in. "Saw me as I came over the first wall."

"But he didn't tell," said Mig lazily. "Doesn't count. We saw nobody, nobody saw us. We got across the road, we got across the meadows, and we're here."

"Clear by Dad's rules." Peter nodded.

They lay peacefully, getting their breath back, pleased with themselves.

Peter was almost ready to drive them on again when Mig said softly, "Freeze!"

The two boys held themselves rigid and Peter whispered apprehensively, "Shepherd?"

"Kestrel," breathed Mig. "Almost above us."

"Birds!" exclaimed Peter in the same tone that he had used earlier when he said, "Girls!" None the less he stayed rigid, looking carefully up into the sky.

The kestrel was hovering perhaps fifteen yards up the slope from them and not more than thirty feet from the ground. They could see the intricate, exquisite movement of its wing feathers, the delicate spread and contraction of its tail as it compensated for the little breeze that came across the ridge. They could even see its eyes as the head moved, following the progress of some invisible prey along the ground.

Peter said, "Sparrowhawk."

It is possible to confuse the birds at times.

"Kestrel!" Mig repeated the word with only the very slightest emphasis. She was placidly certain of her knowledge.

"Hawk!" Clinton thrust in. "They're all hawks to me. What's he after?"

"Fieldmouse or a vole," Mig answered casually. "He's an omen. If he gets it, we get over the Wall. If he misses, we don't."

"And you'd bet on a bird?"

"I'm not betting," Mig countered softly. "The Romans used birds as omens—black crows flying from the left or something—eagles doing things—I can't remember. He'll get what he's after. Look at him!"

The little falcon maintained its vantage, balanced and implacable, utterly sure of itself. They watched, Mig marveling at the superb control of brain and feather. And then suddenly, and even while a sentence of admiration was only half formed, it swooped, gathering speed with one tremendous thrust of its wings, and shot down in a flash of brown against the blue.

Mig wriggled over. There was a brief moment of confusion. A wing flung up. There was a scuffle of feathers, grass waved, and then with a defiant "Kee! Kee!" the kestrel launched itself into the air again, and in its claws was a little bundle of gray, limp and motionless. The bird made a half circle and headed south.

"He's got a nest in the forest," said Mig positively. "We'll get over the Wall, and we'll beat the Prof. The omen"—she sat up abruptly—"the omen has spoken."

"Omens don't speak," said Peter forcefully. "Oracles speak. Omens indicate."

"All right!" Mig looked at her brother. "The omen has indicated." Climbing to her feet, she began to put on her pack.

They came to a fork in the stream, and Peter without hesitation took the left branch and pressed on uphill. They reached a patch of wet peat and bore left again and came out eventually between the two outcrops of the Watch Crags.

Short of the skyline Peter stopped them once more. "Spell-o!" he said a second time. "I'll leave my pack and get on to the Crags and see if there's anything moving."

The other two lay resting lazily. After a little while they were aware of a murmuring noise that continued without interruption but with faint changes of volume. It seemed to have power behind it, as if the sound had almost a weight of its own.

"Something's moving," said Mig. "Let's see how he gets out of this one."

"What is it?"

She listened again for a moment. "Tractor—forestry

tractor, I'd guess. I wonder what he'll compare a forestry tractor with."

"Roman? I'd say a chariot."

"All the way up here over tracks?" demanded Mig. "I'd say a wagon—a wagon getting supplies. A Land-Rover would do for a chariot."

The American boy nodded. "What was the name of your queen that fixed scythe blades to the hubs of her chariots?"

"Boadicea," replied Mig promptly.

"You could have yourself a ball if you fixed scythe blades on the hubs of a jeep."

Peter came down to them, moving silently on the turf. "That was a bit of luck. Five minutes earlier and they'd have got us in the open."

"Tractor?" asked Mig aggravatingly.

"How did you know?" Her brother stared down at her. "Tractor and a Land-Rover. How did you know? Did you go over the skyline?"

"Too obedient," said Clinton, his hat pulled over his eyes. "One military wagon, one chariot."

Peter thought for a moment. "Yes, I suppose for comparison that would be about right. They were going west down the track alongside the slope. There's nobody else moving. We'll be clear at the far end. Let's get going!"

They were on the top of the great ridge now. As they followed Peter over the skyline, they saw suddenly in front of them the long rampart of the Wark forest. To the west it ended abruptly at a point like a promontory on a sea cliff—the land fell away, and far beyond it they could see forest again, dark green altering almost to blue in the distance. To the east it ended in another promontory. Nothing moved in front of them except a wisp of crows circling curiously above something dead on the ground. Peter set a tough pace on the level.

It was hot in the lee of the forest, the faint breeze from the south was cut off here. It was silent too, except for the call of the wood pigeons and the occasional clack of an angry blackbird.

Mig dropped imperceptibly farther and farther behind. Twice Clinton looked round as if to ask if she were all right. Each time she grinned and waved to show that she was. Peter was too occupied with leading to take notice.

When she reckoned she was far enough behind, she slipped one strap of her pack, brought it halfway round and fumbled in the outside pocket. After a minute she pulled out a small transistor radio, hardly bigger than the palm of her hand. It was at the moment her most important possession. Expertly she found the station she needed and held it to her ear.

A thin and carefully modulated voice discussed the problems of housekeeping and a part-time job. Mig accepted the information tranquilly and let it pass. She looked at her watch—it was still a minute and a half short of twelve o'clock.

The voice reached some positive conclusion which she ignored. She looked at her watch again and almost stumbled in the act. A new voice bellowed out a triumphant challenge, and the blast of sound that was the signature tune for which she was waiting swept into the stillness.

Peter flung up his right arm. "Into the bracken! Cover! Into cover . . ."

He flung himself towards the untidy margin of bramble and bracken and rank grass at the edge of the fire break. Clinton flung himself after him. Mig followed sedately.

The signature tune ended as abruptly as it had begun.

There was a brief but absolute silence; then guitars and a trumpet opened with a brash and improbable harmony; and a voice, not thin and carefully modulated this time, stated with rhythmic regret, "She couldn't love me any more . . ."

Peter's head whipped round. His voice, outraged, spluttered, "Mig!"

"It's the Mosspickers," returned Mig placidly.

"I thought . . ."

"You couldn't have thought it was Roman legionaires," she said reasonably.

"Never mind what I thought! I told you we couldn't afford to carry anything extra this trip."

"You aren't." His sister smiled at him. "I am."

He spluttered helplessly, climbing up from the bruised bracken into which he had thrown himself. "I thought we could get away from . . ."

"It's the Mosspickers." Mig's voice put this forward as an elementary fact. "Every day this week at twelve. You couldn't expect me to *miss* the Mosspickers!"

"Turn it down," said Peter hopelessly, and Mig knew that she had won. "Turn it down! Anyone could hear it from half a mile."

She manipulated the milled wheel with her thumb.

"Still farther!" insisted her brother.

Clinton, watching them from the bracken, began to laugh.

"She switches it on in bed in the morning. Under the blankets so's Dad can't hear."

"It's my age," said Mig airily. "I expect I'll grow out of it. You took cover beautifully."

Her brother grunted and settled his rucksack afresh.

Six minutes later they came to the end of the cliff of firs. Peter halted them in cover. "I'll go ahead. We ought to be able to see clear for a mile at least. Mig . . ."

"I've turned it off," she said helpfully. "I'll keep it off till you get back."

Clinton, lying back on his pack, squinted up at her. "Why do you ride him so hard?"

"He gets so serious about things." Mig chuckled wickedly. "If he'd had his way he'd have done this dressed in skins"—she paused and then laughed outright—"or woad or something. I'll keep quiet if there's any danger of anybody hearing, and hide if we have to."

Peter came into sight again round the farther trees. He help up a thumb.

"Okay," said Clinton. "Let's go!"

They carried Peter's pack to him.

He said, pleased with things, "Nothing moving. A few sheep, but they're low down. I think I could spot where the Forestry men were working—there's nobody there now. I was scared that they might have left a working party. This is where the streams begin to run off the moor." He held out the rough map for Clinton to look at. "You can see the trees coming away from the forest."

They turned the spur of the firs and walked into the cool of the little breeze again.

The first stream was easy. Its valley was shallow and dry, and its bed was simple to cross with a skip and a jump.

In the second of the little valleys there was a tongue of trees—birches, mountain ash, and far down towards the main valley, elms. There was also a mildly treacherous peat hag—low ground from which peat had been cut. Peter led them into it at a swinging pace before he discovered what it was. They backtracked out of it not too wet, but warned, and sought another crossing.

The working party was in the third valley, hidden until they were almost on top of it. Peter, in the lead, saw it first and dropped to his knees. Carefully he crept back. "Foresters—we'll have to work round below them."

They backtracked two hundred yards, and covered by the shoulder of the ridge, moved downhill.

The burn fell in a succession of levels linked by brief rapids. They had to find the third level before they could pass in safety. Even there they were held for five anxious minutes by a man eating a vast sandwich with one hand and tossing pebbles down the burn with the other.

"You'd think they were kids!" said Peter scornfully.

Round the next ridge was a farmhouse. Again Peter saw it first and came back, crestfallen. "My fault—I'd forgotten about the farms. I planned to keep close to the forest."

"Right," said Clinton. "Let's get back to it then."

"They'd see us." Peter jerked his thumb towards the men. "If we don't, they'll see us from the farm."

"What about a wall?" Mig's voice was lazy.

"Is there a wall?"

"There's always a wall in Northumberland," she replied.

"Let's look." The American boy glanced at Peter.

"You wait here." Peter slipped his pack.

Mig settled herself, and with the transistor operating at the barest whisper, listened to the Mosspickers contentedly.

They came back after what seemed a long time. "We go on down." Peter nodded down the slope. "There *is* a wall. It runs . . ." He gestured to show its direction. "It meets another wall above the farm, and we'll have to watch our chance and get across that. Then we keep in cover behind the second wall, and it takes us almost to the farmyard. If we can get past there, we're all right. There's cover beyond and then a shoulder of hill. We'll have to go fast and quietly."

The first two walls gave them no problem, but as they moved down towards the farmhouse, they saw that there was a gate into the field which they had not yet reached. It was Mig who saw the dog through the gate. All three of them froze in their tracks at her word. The dog ambled slowly across the gap and disappeared.

"If he's one of those sheep dogs," whispered Clinton, "we got no more chance'n a snowball in . . ." He bit off the quotation.

"Hell," whispered Mig behind him, rounding it off. "He's a sheep dog all right, but he's old—the way he moves. He's a yard dog now."

"C'n still bark," said Clinton.

Peter searched for a higher stone in the wall, raised his head cautiously to it, and made a hurried sweep of the back of the farm. Chickens scratched peacefully. Three doves sat in a row on the ridge of a shed. A thin wisp of smoke showed above a kitchen chimney. It was utterly sleepy. He crouched down again. "Wind's right for us. He looks lazy, and he's probably deaf. What are you doing?"

Mig had her pack off and was crouched over it. She pulled out a package in greaseproof paper, unwrapped it, and drew out a half-cooked sausage. "If he doesn't hear us till we're close to him, chuck him this when he barks. Never knew a farm dog that wouldn't stop to look at a bit of meat."

Peter put the sausage in his handkerchief.

"Right," said Mig. "If you don't use it, *you* eat it. It's your handkerchief."

They went on, moving even more cautiously, quite silent on the sheep-cropped turf. The angle of the wall prevented any sight of the dog. Clearly he had found himself some comfortable patch of sun. At the gate they studied the back windows of the farmhouse warily. There was no sign of life. One by one they tiptoed over the sun-baked mud at the gateway and gained the shelter of the wall beyond. They were almost clear when the dog barked. Peter fumbled at the handkerchief.

Mig said urgently, "Wait!" The next bark seemed farther away; the third was unquestionably so; and there was another noise with it. Her hearing was acute. "Land-Rover coming up to the farm. Scoot!"

The dog went off barking across the yard. By the time the noise stopped the three were clear and in the shelter of a patch of scrub two hundred yards from the house.

"Give me back the sausage," said Mig placidly. "I'll mark it."

4

Miss Kirton looked up over her shoulder. She was hot and red, and two locks of hair were stuck to her forehead against the line of the curl. "That's that! There's nothing more we can do tonight." She brought out a last careful handful of earth.

Professor Carrick accepted her declaration reluctantly. The September sun was still high, but seven of his team had to get back to Newcastle and the nearest were billeted at Hexham. He said, "I suppose so."

Miss Kirton straightened herself. "We still won't be able to shift it." She flicked a finger against the rim of the dish. "The other stone's pinning it about seven inches up, I'm sure of that. There's no clearance at all. But at least we'll be able to see the base of it." She turned squarely to the Professor. "I oughtn't to say it, I know, and it's possible that it's just a series of normal grooves and crosses, but I'm almost certain there's lettering underneath *this*." She looked down at the stone.

"There could be. It's part of a lintel."

"Suppose it's a dated inscription?"

"That," replied the Professor severely, "is wishful thinking, Miss Kirton."

They both laughed.

He walked down to the center of the ditch. "Closing time, ladies and gentlemen!"

"Seventeen and a half minutes after closing time," said one of the young men cheerfully, and added, "Slave driver!"

Witton came over. "I wouldn't mind staying on for another hour."

Two or three of the others murmured agreement.

Carrick said, "No, it's been a good day; the pattern's beginning to come clearer, I think. There's no need to rush things. I'd like to be able to determine the end of the fire area by tomorrow. D'you think that will be possible?"

"I don't see why not," answered Witton. "It isn't more than a foot or so from the point we've reached."

"The whole of the east wall must have fallen in one piece and smothered it." One of the older men put forward the suggestion hesitantly.

"We'll know in a day or two," said Carrick. "Shall we get the stuff down to my car?"

The day's finds, wrapped and ticketed, were in trays: a broken Samian bowl, complete in all its fragments, that could undoubtedly be pieced together again; a glass vial, fire-damaged and melted out of shape; three doubtful pieces of iron; a bronze knife hilt; a piece of silver so encrusted that it was impossible to identify it without cleaning; a clay votive offering, eroded by water through the ruins, that might once have been an arm; a whole series of shards of pottery, scarred and broken from the fire zone.

They were already certain that the western end of the house had burned fiercely. It was not yet possible to be certain that the collapse of the eastern end had checked it, but there was no fire in the area about the great dish. As far down as they had been able to get at the earth between the blocks that pinned it, there was no charcoal, no blackening. The possibilities of this were very clear in Carrick's mind. As far as it was possible for him to permit it, he was elated.

He supervised the movement of the day's finds calmly, however. They were storing the specimens at the Housesteads Museum, three quarters of a mile along the slope. He gave his keys to Witton. "Two of you go with him! Drop them at the cars and come back for the rest of us." He had stopped the others bringing their cars up to the site to avoid attracting attention. They were parked now on the verge of the Carlisle road. Notices had been put up well clear of the area: "Excavation. Private. Visitors apply at Housesteads Museum." And Housesteads Museum was instructed to say, "No visitors." It would not keep everybody away, the Professor acknowledged morosely, but it would keep some of 'em.

He went back to the section where the great dish still lay tight-held between the fallen ashlar and watched the team putting light timbers across and spreading a protective plastic sheet for the night. When it was done, he settled himself on a convenient stone and began to light his pipe. "Who's guard for the night?"

"Prentice," replied one of the girls.

Over his shoulder he asked, "Prentice, will you be all right or do you want somebody else with you?"

"Absolutely all right," said Prentice.

5

The afternoon was suddenly dark as the trees closed round them. So far they had avoided the forest, but at this point Peter planned to use it to escape the long haul round Black Law.

From the Watergate Farm they had come without risk to the Blackaburn. At the Blackaburn they had hidden while two men went past with guns, looking apparently for pigeon. They had eaten lunch where they hid, giggling as they watched the men. From Blackaburn they had cut up the wide gap between the arms of the forest past Stonehaugh, using walls and scrub and occasional stretches of dead ground.

All in all, it was a good performance. Peter had proved that he had a real eye for country. Clinton followed respectfully. Neither he nor Mig realized how relieved the elder boy had been to find the sign for the Pennine Way heading between the trees.

Mig was relieved for other reasons. She said unashamedly, "I'm glad to get inside. I was getting goose pimples down my back in the open there. There were eyes everywhere." She paused, wondering at herself for a moment before she repeated, "Everywhere."

Peter said, "We made it, didn't we? And don't reckon on this being safe—it isn't! This path is used. It's the Pennine Way."

"What's that mean?" demanded Clinton.

"It means you can walk just about two hundred and fifty miles of England without using roads. It keeps along the high ground from the Peak in Derbyshire. If you hear voices or see anything through the trees, get off the path and freeze!"

A dove so close above them that its call was almost explosive summoned its mate. Mig answered it instantly: "Tak-two-doo! Tak-two-doo!"

"You might warn me!" Clinton complained.

They went ahead again in single file. The forest was full of small noises, rustlings in the undergrowth, crows wrangling at a high nesting place, red squirrels chattering—friendly noises, pleasant hot-afternoon noises. The air was held still between the trees, and the sounds seemed to penetrate and spread up along mysterious tunnels.

The neck of the woods at this point was roughly a mile across. They were almost three quarters of the way through it before they saw a sign of human life. Clinton spotted the man first—he was temporarily in the lead. They were practiced already in ducking out of sight. Barely six feet from the edge of the path they found at once a hiding place of tall bracken and fallen branches. The man came slowly down the path. In full view of them he stopped and lifted up a heavy pair of binoculars. Mig squeezed her brother's arm.

He whispered, covered by the cooing of the doves, "One of your bird watchers."

The man was elderly, gray-haired. He wore an old-fashioned hunting jacket and corduroys. He lowered his glasses and stood thoughtfully, scratching one ear. Then he came on again and stopped not more than nine feet from them. He put his hands in his pockets and stamped round in a circle, apparently angrily. They heard him say, "Damn' cushats!" He was staring upward all the time, trying to look up to the pinnacles of the trees. Presently he used his binoculars again. Then he dropped them back on his chest, ran his hand under his nose, and sniffed. Finally he strode on crossly down the path.

Mig rolled over and lay there, helpless with suppressed laughter. They watched the man go into a bend of the path and disappear. Mig was still laughing soundlessly. When they got back to the path she said, "I'm going to give up bird watching and watch grown-ups. They mayn't be so beautiful, but they're funnier."

For no particular reason they began to hurry, moving fast down the path and laughing as they ran.

There was a complication at the far end. Peter had told them of it before, but they stopped again, close to the edge of the trees where the blue of the sky began to show through the gaps between the branches, to try to work it out. On this great southern face of the forest there was a fire tower. Peter had no notion as to how it was manned, but he guessed that in the middle of this dry September there would be someone there all day. It was built on the Bell Crags, the highest point in the whole southern sector of the forest. Even with the map Peter had been unable to plan a route that would enable them to escape the fire watchers' eyes. This was the last lap now. It would, of course, be possible to keep in the forest until dusk, but after dusk it would be difficult to find a camping place for the night.

"First thing is to spot the tower. After that we can judge cover," said Peter. "We've got to be careful while we do it, because people will be heading up the Way over open country from this patch." He indicated the detached area

of plantation on Haughton Common. "We want to get"—
he stabbed his pencil point at a corner of the area—"there.
If we go along the north face, they'll see us for a dead certainty. If we go along the south, there are two farms. If
we cut through it, it's two miles along a well-used path."

He went forward alone to the gate at the edge of the
forest. Peering out, he covered the wide open moor ahead.
Far down the path there was a group of three people, moving south. Well over to the east was a scattered flock of
sheep grazing peacefully. No shepherd showed, no dog. He
went out hesitantly into the sun; the forest edge was clear as
far as he could see—so was the fire tower. He nipped back
again smartly.

"Fire tower?" asked Clinton instantly.

"Full view."

"What," demanded Clinton, "do we do next?"

They sat down to think it over, ears cocked for the
possibility of enemy behind them.

Clinton said, "Are you sure there's anyone in the tower?"

"Nope." Peter shook his head. "I didn't stay to find out,
but there will be. Mig, you've got the best eyes. When you
get through the gate, there's some high scrub. Go and sit in
that, and bird watch!"

"How do I get to it?"

"On your stomach," replied her brother unfeelingly.

She was out and back in a minute and a half. "Two," she
said simply. "There didn't seem any point in staying to try
to see the color of their hair at a mile and a half. They were
moving about."

Clinton looked at her admiringly. "You didn't get their
ages?"

"Yank!" retorted the girl scornfully.

Peter asked, "D'you think they spotted me? Should we
count it as an enemy sighting?"

"How far out did you go?"

"Just clear of the gate. There's some high stuff at the side."

"Enough to hide more than half of you," conceded the girl, "and you weren't there more than a second or two."

"Bobbed out and back. I looked south and east first, but I wasn't in line with the tower then."

"Your head and shoulders at a mile and a half . . ." Mig considered the question dispassionately. "Dad wouldn't have counted it."

"Alleesame," asked Clinton, "how do we get out?"

"We don't," said Peter.

"What do we do, then—wait for dark?"

"Wouldn't find our sleeping place then . . ."

"So?"

Peter gestured irritably. "Let me think!" He stared at the rough plan that he had drawn in the morning, trying to visualize the ordnance map. The detached bulk of the Greenlee plantation was linked by a single line to the main forest. He said abruptly, "I wonder!"

"What?" demanded Mig.

"I put it in without thinking, but I remember that the ordnance map showed a tongue of trees joining Greenlee and the big forest. It's wildly close to the fire tower, but there might be enough cover to get by."

"And how do we get to it?" Clinton pointed to the sunlight beyond the trees. "Not thataway—'the natives are hostile.'" He managed a fair parody of an English accent.

"Through the forest."

"You said . . ." Mig's forehead wrinkled.

"I know what I said!" Peter flared out at his sister.

"Use your bean." Mig imitated her father's voice. "We could try it and mark the paths we use."

"How?"

"Hansel and Gretel used peas."

"Yeah, look what happened to them!" Clinton mocked her.

"And"—Mig disregarded the interruption—"we'll use scraps of paper at every intersection to show the way we've come, and at least we'll be able to get back here if things go wrong."

"Brain!" said Clinton with admiration.

"If we take the turnings to the left, one of them's bound to get us back to the southern edge of the forest." Peter took command again.

"Sounds reasonable." Clinton nodded. "Let's go!"

The first intersection was barely a hundred and twenty yards from the forest gate. Mig had remembered it and was ready with a strip of paper from the bird book. She tucked it securely in the bark of a tree. The turning was a cul-de-sac. They went back to the main path and tried the next. This was wider, more used. Two hundred yards along, there was a promising left turn. Peter's eyes brightened. The new path faded out in a small area of young growth. The fourth disappeared for no reason at all almost before it had begun. The fifth shook even Peter.

It was Clinton who said as they plodded silently along its angular changes of course, "Guess it isn't important in this country, but the sun's right behind us now."

"We're heading east then." Mig looked back at him, exasperated.

He grinned at her but said nothing.

The path had come round in a wide, slow sweep, and the next intersection they reached headed due north.

"Now what?" Mig glared at her brother.

"Got to stick to the plan," said Peter stubbornly. "If we don't, we're lost. Mark it!"

The new path kept north for a bare eighty yards, turned

west again abruptly, and almost at once ran into a much-used track that trended toward the south. There were Land-Rover tire marks in it and the cross-hatching of tractor wheels.

"Main drag!" exploded Clinton triumphantly.

They went down it fast, relieved of the oppression of the forest.

The edge came suddenly; they were unprepared for it. Peter held them back with a gesture of both hands, saying warningly, "The tower first." They crept forward. To the left a small crag heaved out of the forest; level with it the track ran into a clearing. Above it and to the right was the Bell Crags tower. Well down the track was the tongue of trees that Peter had believed joined the main forest. It ended abruptly in open moor.

"Somebody," murmured Mig sweetly, "has been misreading his map."

Clinton said over his shoulder, "Younger sisters are murdered by millions every year."

Peter said humbly, "I misread it all right. I thought it connected up."

They sat in the half-shelter of a patch of bracken and studied the area disconsolately.

It was Clinton who spoke first. "How high d'you reckon that clump of whatever-you-call-it with the thorn bush is?" His finger pointed to a patch of scrub.

Mig said distantly, "You mean the little rowan in the middle. Four feet." And then maliciously, "Four foot six."

"Okay," said the American boy pacifically. "I calc'late it's halfway across. This"—he gestured at the ridge of the crag—"should cover all 'cept about a hundred and fifty yards. That means we got to have time enough to sprint seventy-five yards while they're both looking the other way."

"But . . ."

The American boy raised his hand. "Mig goes up on to the ridge an' crawls till she can see that tower thing. We go along on to the level until *we* can see it, an' she signals—hand or hank'chief or somethin'—when we're in the clear, and one of us makes an end run to the clump. Then she waits for another chance, and we both watch her, and when she signals again, the one at the clump makes a run for the trees and the other one runs for the clump."

"And Mig?" Peter demanded keenly.

"She comes down to the level then, an' the one at the clump signals, and she makes her run for it while he goes for the trees. Then she judges her own last run."

"It would be fairer if one of us . . ."

"Nuts! She's got better eyes 'n either of us."

Mig felt happily warm.

"We'll take your pack for you."

Clinton said, "No, we won't! We've got enough to carry for a sprint ourselves. She can manage."

Mig felt happier still.

Peter said, "We'll take it as far as the starting point, and that'll mark it for you when you come down from the ridge."

"You do that!" Mig's voice was bubbling.

She began to work along the ridge without further word. When it started to slope away at the end, she crouched and moved upward. Finally she was flat on her stomach, wriggling. There was a patch of thistles on the skyline. She came up behind the clump, parted the stems, and looked out. Involuntarily she said aloud, "Glory be!" One of the men was climbing down the ladder from the platform. She glanced behind to see if she could see the boys, but they had not yet found a point where they could see her and were at the same time close enough to the clump. The watcher who was left leaned over the edge, calling down to his friend. She could hear his voice faintly. Presently, the other man having, she guessed, disappeared, he moved to the southern edge of the platform and leaned there with his arms on the rail. Behind her, well down the slope, Peter's head came into view. She turned and held up one thumb. Peter held up his own thumb in return. She lay there, watching. The man seemed comfortably settled for the evening; he made no move at all. The thistles began to prick her legs, and an ant crawled over her arm. She blew it away. As if the man had seen the movement, he stood back from the rail and took a pair of binoculars from somewhere below him. When he steadied himself, however, he was looking due south, not eastward to their position, concentrating on something across the valley of the Great Whin Sill.

She put out her handkerchief. It had been agreed that she would lift it when she thought that an opportunity was coming and flag it down when she meant the first runner to start. The watcher put the strap of the binoculars over his head and stood a minute longer, looking south. Then he went to the western side of the tower. Mig's arm shot up with the handkerchief. She hoped the boys were still watching, but she dared not take her eyes from the tower. She held it up for a long half minute to make certain. The watcher lifted the binoculars, and at once her hand went down, the handkerchief fluttering. Desperately she wanted to watch the runner, but she knew that she dared not. The man stood sweeping the western moor. Finally, satisfied about whatever it was that he was watching, he dropped the glasses. Mig wriggled herself round. There was no sign of anyone at the rowan clump, but the head that she saw down the slope was Clinton's, not Peter's. She put one thumb up again, and Clinton's hand shot up with his thumb outstretched.

So far, so good. She turned to watch the tower again. The watcher was facing north. Once again he lifted the binoculars. Once again Mig's hand shot up with the handkerchief, fluttered for a moment and came down. She lay thinking: He'll come to the east end now and go through the same performance and then go south; I've plenty of time.

She wriggled backwards until she was clear, and then moved down the slope. Her rucksack was resting in a clear patch, plain to see. When she reached it, she could see the back of Clinton's head and half his arm behind the rowan. He was clearly staring at the tower. She slipped on the rucksack and waited. It was like waiting for the starting gun in a race. Her heart was beating idiotically fast; her face was hot. This was the final test.

Even as she acknowledged that, there was a flutter of white behind the rowan, and she began to run. Simultaneously Clinton lifted to his full height and moved away. She raced as fast as she could ever remember having run, the pack thumping on her back. It seemed incredibly farther than it had been when they first tried to judge the distance. She knew that she couldn't make it before the watcher came to the southern rail again. Clinton had given the signal too early anyway; he must have. But she couldn't look at the tower. The ground was rough, uneven; she had to watch her footing. And then suddenly, without any certainty as to the last few yards, she was behind the rowan, her breath wheezing and her whole body hot and on fire. When she was able to focus on the tower, the watcher was at the western end again, staring with the binoculars at something in the direction of Spadeadam Waste.

She got her breath back before he moved. The glasses were dropped. She thought, He's bound to come to the south face now, and settled herself to wait. But he went instead to the northwest corner, and suddenly with enormous determination she got to her feet again and ran blindly to the trees. After a long—an impossibly long—period she heard a voice: "Here, Mig! Here!" The trees were suddenly above her, and she saw Clinton holding out his hand. She collapsed, wheezing, and let the pack slip off her shoulders.

Clinton said, "Good girl! Good girl!"

Peter came back, his face a broad grin. "He's still looking to the west. Good work, Mig! We've beaten 'em."

Half an hour later they came out, after one false lead, at the western tip of the Greenlee wood. Peter made the usual careful reconnaissance. There was not a sign of life anywhere ahead of them. Immediately below the point where the path emerged there was a stream.

"The Greenlee burn," said Peter solemnly. "I never thought we'd make it. Come on out! It's all right. We're in dead ground here. They can't see us. Here's where we camp."

He led up the shallow hollow in which the stream ran. In a hundred yards he found what he was looking for—a flat clearing of turf between high clumps of rushes. It had been cropped down by the grazing sheep to an almost lawnlike smoothness.

He dropped his pack wearily. "Call it a day!"

"Will do," said Clinton promptly, and dropped his own. "Where's this Wall of yours?"

Peter laughed. The relief in his laughter was apparent to the other two. "Come on, then!" and he ran forward up the easy slope. "That'll be the Sweet Rigg ahead of us. I remember it clearly now. I've got it fixed. As long as we keep behind it, we're all right." He looked back to make sure that the fire tower had not risen suddenly over the ridge to the northeast. For another hundred yards he went on. They were coming close to the skyline. At length he stopped.

"Easy now! We've just about made it." He took another ten paces forward and said proudly, "There!"

The whole wide valley below the Great Whin Sill was golden in the afternoon sun. The loughs in the bottom were a Mediterranean blue, beyond Crag Lough the red-black cliffs lifted like an angry barricade. To the west the survivors of the Nine Nicks of Thirlwall were like a saw edge against the sky. To the east the Hotbank Crags soared and fell and soared again. At the farthest end of their view the softer slopes of Housesteads fell away against the blue. Along them, linking crag to crag and height to height, the Wall ran golden, picked out by the sun, heightened by some magic of the light once again into the rampart that it had been, menacing and magnificent.

6

Two ravens flew into their line of sight, little more than level with them but high above the valley floor. One of them tripped, apparently over his own wings, and fell tumbling in the ravens' play. The other circled. They flew on again, and across the stillness came a derisive "Kronk!" They disappeared toward the sunset.

"Right!" said Peter happily. "Let's make camp."

"Who sets up my tent for me?" demanded Clinton.

"You do!"

"*Uh*-uh! Mig explained it all to me. No one could pitch it after that."

They came back to their packs and started to unstrap the light tent rolls. Clinton spread his out on the soft turf.

"It's a bedding roll," he said at length. He hefted it in one hand. "Can't be a tent!"

"Watch!" Mig spread her roll flat on the patch she had chosen. From a pocket at the foot she withdrew four aluminum pegs. "So—and so!" She pushed one peg through each of the two rings at the bottom corners, crawled to the far end, stretched the length of the roll, and put in pegs at the opposite corners.

"Pegged-down bedding roll," said Clinton firmly. "No tent."

From the pocket Mig withdrew two aluminum tubes with spike ends. Fumbling inside the tent itself, she found a socket for each, thrust the spike through an eyelet set in the material, and rammed it at an angle into the earth. She repeated the same on the other side. From the sockets she stretched out a length of thin nylon line and fastened it round the stem of a heather clump on either side.

"Tent," she announced shortly. "Weight, with bedding, three and a half pounds. Dad's own invention. Possible if you use waterproof nylon."

Clinton sat rocking on his heels. "Your dad's got something. And the sleeping bag?"

"Three layers of nylon," replied Mig promptly. "You use one if it's a hot night, two if it's cold. The tent keeps the wind off, and that's what matters."

"Sure that's what matters." Clinton grunted approvingly, walking round the erection with a solemn face. "Your mother made it? I take off my hat. If I freeze tonight, I freeze respectfully."

Behind him Peter laughed. "You won't freeze. You might be too hot. It's the nylon that does it."

The two went on with their preparations methodically. It was plain that they had had abundant experience. Behind Peter, Mig was looking for a flat patch of rock in the stream bed to take the solid-fuel stove.

She heard Clinton say, "Blast! It looked so simple."

"Dad says it needs only common intelligence."

"*Thank* you!" Clinton's voice was injured.

Peter walked over to him. "Shall I lend you a hand?"

"G'way! Beat it! Scat! I'll do it if it busts me!"

Mig extracted a lightweight frying-pan from a waterproof

case. Without fuss she lit the stove, put a knob of butter in the pan, and started to heat it.

"Peg's struck a rock," said Clinton's voice behind her.

"Draw one of the bottom pegs and shift it around till all four go in. Show him, Pete!"

"G'way! I'll do it myself."

Mig had got the sausages into the pan before a triumphant bellow announced that success had been achieved. She said patronizingly, "Actually done it?" And then, referring to the sausage that Peter had harbored in his handkerchief to placate the sheep dog, "The mark's disappeared, but I don't suppose it'll matter. You haven't got a cold anyway."

"Pig!" said her brother distantly.

There was light enough from the long northern twilight for them to finish their meal and for Mig to prepare a great beaker of chocolate. In the half-darkness they sat around drinking it.

The south wind had dropped utterly. The night was very still with, underneath the stillness, a muted pattern of bird noises—owls in the forest, nightjars, and a faint plaintive piping that Mig could not identify and chose to be aggrieved about. Occasionally they heard feather whispers overhead and once the harp music of swans' wings.

It was when this had died away that Clinton said, "Now, tell!"

"Tell what?"

"About this Wall."

Mig peered closely at him in the starlight. "Of course, you wouldn't know about it! I never thought of that. We should have explained. We've been brought up with it. You've just come along on trust?"

"You could say that—again."

"Good boy!" said Mig, collecting her revenge for the race across the open. "Good boy!"

Peter asked, "What do you want to know?"

"Everything for a start—and just what you're really aiming to do, for a finish."

Mig lay back lazily on the turf. "I think he must have a nice character."

"Shut up!" ordered her brother. "Where d'you want me to begin?"

"Who built it, would do."

Mig laughed.

Peter said unhappily, "I thought you'd ask that. It's about the most difficult question of the lot."

"It's called Hadrian's Wall, isn't it?" asked Clinton reasonably. "Didn't he build it, then?"

"Hadrian was emperor when it was built. He came to Britain about the time it was started, but it isn't as easy as all that."

"How come?"

Peter sat silent for a minute, trying to shape his answer. "Actually there were two plans for the wall. Dad says one of them's Hadrian's. The trouble is which."

"What do the experts say?"

"They just say Hadrian's."

"Okay. What's your Dad's point?"

Peter did not answer the question directly. Instead he said, "When Hadrian became emperor, the Romans were being pushed down out of Scotland. He sent over a pal of his called Nepos, Aulus Platorius Nepos, as legate—governor, if you like. Dad says he must have told him to stop the rot."

"How?"

"Probably ordered him to choose a frontier and hold it— or else! Anyway, somebody—and it was most likely Nepos —planned a wall from the Tyne to the Solway."

"Why?"

"It's the shortest line across the north of England. But

Dad says that there was a lot more to it than that. For one thing, it was the northern end of the country of a big tribe called the Brigantes, and the Brigantes were friends with the Romans then. For another"—he waved a hand in the starlight to cover the south—"he could run his line along the top of the Great Whin Sill."

"The what?"

"You saw it from the top this evening—the escarpment —the cliffs." Again his hand sketched an arc to the south. "It's an outcrop of hard whinstone that runs just about the whole length of the middle bit of the Wall."

"It would be tough to rush it?" Clinton suddenly saw the possibilities.

"You'd have to attack up the slope," answered Peter. "You couldn't attack up the cliffs at all. The Romans could hold it with a handful of men for a short time—they could see any attack coming a long way off."

"So this Nepos character built it?"

"Not exactly." Again Peter hesitated. "He planned it and he started it."

"How long was it?" Clinton's mind reached out in an effort to grasp the thing as a whole.

"Seventy-six Roman miles from the bridge they built across the Tyne at Newcastle to Bowness below the last ford on the Solway, eighty miles after they added the bit to Wallsend. A Roman mile was one thousand six hundred and twenty yards—call it seventy-three and a half English miles."

Clinton whistled. "That long?"

"It was, and it was fifteen foot six high to the patrol walk and the battlements were six feet above that, and it was nine foot six thick. There was a mile-castle every mile to hold fifty men, and there were turrets between the mile-castles."

"That," said Clinton soberly, "sounds as if it was quite a

48

project." He examined it silently while the other two waited. Suddenly he asked, "And they reckoned they could hold it with fifty men to the mile?"

Mig said, "Good for you, Clint! That's the point."

Peter said, "Yes. I wish Dad was here to explain it. I know what he means, but it isn't easy to make it clear. Dad says it wasn't a static wall."

"Come again?"

"I think he means that it wasn't just a wall that they stood behind and defended. For one thing, there was a gate at every mile-castle through the Wall to the north. He says it was designed from the start for the offensive/defensive." He reeled off the military jargon phrase with the ease of familiarity.

"Explain!"

"It means, I think, that the Wall was there to cover a sort of military area and that the Romans concentrated troops behind it when they guessed that there was an attack coming down and shot them out fast through whichever gates suited them so that they could counterattack the tribes on their flanks and break 'em up before they reached the Wall."

"I know!" Clinton's voice was keen. "But what sort of counterattack could you set up with fifty men to the mile?"

"I hadn't got to that yet. Dad says the Wall garrison was a patrol garrison—just that. As far as anybody knows, the first plan was to put the real fighting garrisons in the forts that Agricola—he was another legate—built forty years earlier down in the valley of the Tyne. And the whole thing depended on the legions at Chester in the west and York on the east anyway. If an attack was too big for the local garrisons, they could get the legions up from Chester in five days or in two and a half from York."

"Big deal!" exclaimed Clinton. "What happened?"

"They started to build it. They dug the ditch; they laid the foundations from Newcastle to the Irthing—that's a river ten miles to the west of here. And they started to build the Wall . . . then they stopped."

"Why?"

"Plan changed."

"Who changed it?"

"Dad says only the emperor could have changed it. That's why he's certain that Nepos made the first plan. He says only Hadrian could have given the orders to stop such a damn expensive piece of work and fill in a ditch that they'd just finished digging and pull down stonework they'd just started to put up."

"What did they do instead?"

"Redesigned the whole thing to put the garrisons on the line of the Wall itself and built whacking great forts clean across it, with about a third of 'em sticking out to the north of it and three more gates, wide enough to take chariots, in the part that stuck out."

"How big were they?"

"Five acres—more. They had barracks and granaries and stables, and a whacking great headquarters building with a chapel of the legions and a court with columns round it, and a house for the garrison commander with his own bath and central heating and all. Dad says he calculates it must have just about bust the British treasury."

"And he reckons the emperor did it?"

"He says *only* the emperor would have had the nerve."

"Why?"

"Somebody 'underestimated the threat.'" He used the modern military term.

"Meaning?"

"Didn't see that the Caledonians, or whatever they were called, were tougher than the first plan allowed for."

"Where do we fit in?"

Mig said, "The Prof's always talking about the Wall bein' designed to stop infiltration."

"That means . . ." began Peter.

"I know. It's the big thing in guerrilla war." Clinton nodded. "Right! What do *we* prove?"

"I keep forgetting." Peter looked over apologetically. "You weren't there for the argument. We'd done most of the fighting with Dad before you came—days of it!"

"He didn't think it could be done?"

"Oh, no!" Mig chipped in. "He's as certain as we are, but takes the other side so's to be sure we don't forget anything important."

Clinton laughed. "So does mine."

"There are two parts to it." Peter stuck to his explanation. "Getting here was the first part. I said if we could get to the Wall without being seen that was half the battle. We're here anyway."

"Right!"

"Getting over it's the other half." He paused for a minute and they were all silent, remembering the long solid line of the Wall in the afternoon sun. "We think you could get three people over—five, perhaps—without being spotted."

"How?"

"The whole thing depends on the turrets," said Peter slowly. "Two of them, I told you, between each two mile-castles. That puts 'em a third of a Roman mile apart—about five hundred and forty yards, say. There were four men to a turret—five at the most—and when a watch was being kept they must have worked them two on and two off. Fine weather it'd have been all right. They could've watched from the turrets along most of the Wall, but not along the crags here. Dad says the Romans' minds were too tidy. They spaced 'em just about equally, and there are lots of places where they couldn't have seen over the next ridge. They'd have had to keep up a regular patrol there, and they'd have had to keep up a patrol everywhere in thick weather—fog or snow or rain even. With four men to a turret, you'd have two men off and one man out on the Wall each side of the turret, and he'd walk up to meet the man from the next turret and walk back again."

He paused, visualizing the patrol in his mind.

"They'd walk out, and they'd meet in the middle, and they'd have a natter—sentries always natter when the sergeant isn't looking—and they'd turn, and they'd go back as far as the turret. Not fast—you don't move fast when you've got to do it all over again and again and again—say, three miles an hour, perhaps less—eighty yards a minute. Each man would have to do two hundred and seventy yards —call it three minutes or three and a half even. Three minutes with both sentries' backs toward the middle." He stopped.

Clinton said quickly, "You've got to get up to the foot of the Wall, swing your grapnel up, make certain it holds, shin up it, and get over in three minutes." His voice was skeptical.

"That's it." Peter nodded eagerly in the darkness. "You can—we've proved it . . ."

"How?"

"With the boat grapnel. It wasn't popular!" Mig giggled. "Dad didn't know about it until we had just about a minute to go before the ten-minute gun for a race and he wanted the grapnel."

"Dinghy race," Peter explained. "You've got to be clear of your moorings ten minutes before the start."

Mig took it up again. "When I gave it to him he said, 'What in Tophet's this?' and I said, 'Wolf hide,' because I was still thinking of it that way—and he blew his top!"

"Translate!" demanded Clinton.

"Well"—Peter considered his explanation—"we'd been talking about it a lot, and we reckoned that if you heaved a grapnel up on to a stone parapet it would land with an almighty clank and even a sleepy sentry'd hear it. So we guessed that they'd have padded it with sheepskin or something, and Mig said wolf hide'd be better, and we used some special canvas that Dad had hidden away and he was mad." After a brief pause he added, "Naturally." He paused again. "Tophet's Hebrew for hell, far as I can remember."

"And did you win the race?" asked Clinton unexpectedly.

"Came in fourth," said Mig.

Clinton began to splutter with laughter. Finally he asked, "What happened next?"

"We'd sewed the canvas padding round the flukes, and we used the roof of the boat shed—it was about eighteen foot—to try it. Didn't make a bit of noise. After the first tries I could land it five times out of six. 'Tisn't difficult really. We nailed pieces of wood to the top of the wall to mark the crenel."

"The what?"

"Battlements." Peter sketched the alternation of battlements in the starlight. "The standing-up part's the merlon, the cut-out part's the crenel. You took cover behind the merlon, and you fired arrows out across the crenel, or if they put scaling ladders up, you used your sword through it. The ledge was about three feet above the patrol path."

"And you climbed up the rope?"

"You run up the wall really. We did it best in bare feet. You grab the rope as high as you can. You put your feet up against the wall, and you pull yourself up."

"You too, Mig?"

"I wasn't as quick as he was," said Mig modestly. "We don't do so much gym at school. It isn't difficult once you get the knack of it. We *were* best with bare feet. They probably used rawhide sandals."

"What on earth did your dad say when he found out?"

"Oh, he was all right," Mig answered tolerantly. "He got interested. He made us try it out with a stopwatch after the race. Even when he found out about the guttering, he was so interested he didn't mind."

"The guttering?"

"The fluke of the grapnel caught in it once, and we didn't notice it till I was halfway up," explained Peter reluctantly. "It came away. But he was being very scientific about timing us when he discovered it, so it didn't matter."

"How often do you two get away with murder?"

"Quite often," said Mig cheerfully.

"What sort of time did it take?"

"I averaged thirty-three seconds from heaving the grapnel." Peter was exact. "Dad gave us a minute to get from a hiding place where we could wait in safety to the Wall, thirty-five seconds across the Wall, three seconds down the other side, and thirty seconds each for the men that followed. He reckoned that gave us about nine seconds' grace. We had to get out of sight in that time."

"Could do," said Clinton, "but you'd need luck."

"We'd need it," acknowledged Peter.

"And if you had five men?"

"They'd have used two grapnels." Peter nodded. "I don't think you could get away with more than five and not be seen."

"Supposing you had to?"

"Then I don't think you'd do it without forty men."

"Why?"

"You'd never get enough men across while the sentries' backs were turned, and they'd give the alarm."

"How?"

"By shouting. There *are* stories about speaking tubes along the Wall, but Dad says they're a lot of nonsense. One pair of lungs was enough to carry from one patrol to the next."

"How *would* you have got forty men across, then?"

"You'd have had to take out the two men on patrol first thing—take 'em from behind," said Peter firmly. "Then, if you could get the off-duty men in the turret, and maybe the two men patrolling the other side of it, by surprise, you'd have time to get clear."

"*If* . . ." Clinton emphasized the word.

"If you didn't," said Peter promptly, "you'd have to fight off the garrison of one mile-castle."

"Fifty men?"

"Uh-huh. I said they were designed for fifty men. Most of them never had barracks for more than twenty-five. Mile-castle 37—that's the one we'll be nearest to—probably didn't have more'n twenty. Even if somebody sprang the alarm, they wouldn't have had to face more than a dozen or so fresh men because eight would have been on duty in the turrets anyway. They'd have planned to move toward the weakest castle. The next garrison, even if it got the alarm at the same time, would be best part of three quarters of a mile behind 'em. They'd have finished off the first garrison and been well down the slope into the Tyne Forest before the forts could have sent out a force big enough to take care of them."

"And you worked this all out by yourselves?" demanded Clinton.

Peter shook his head vigorously. "Dad helped."

Mig said, "He's got a bet on us."

"How much?"

"Dunno—but we'll get it out of him in the end."

7

A pleasant morning smell of bacon and beans and coffee drifted down the slope. Prentice waved a fork at Carrick. "Mornin', Prof. Could I offer you a cup of coffee? Run to a plate of beans if you're desperate."

Carrick grunted. "Any trouble in the night?"

"Nary a trouble. I overslept, that's all."

"Hear anything?"

"Cars on the road, and those crazy swans from the Crag Lough flighting around."

"Splendid!" Almost automatically, Carrick looked up into the cloudless morning sky. "Done any work?"

"Me union says 'No breakfast, no work.' I've taken off the covers, that's all."

Carrick strolled over to the trench where the edge of the dish showed very clear in the morning sun.

"It's still there," said Prentice with a grin. "Honestly, it was a quiet night. I kept awake till dawn, and then I dozed with my head out of the door of the shed. Wasn't a soul about. I heard the dogs over at the Housesteads farm once. There was nothing else." He looked down the slope beyond the Professor. Miss Kirton and one of the other girls were coming up. The third car was parking beside the Carlisle road. He walked over with his plate in his hand. "I've been studying it. I'd start with this one." He indicated a squared stone with his toe. "Doesn't seem to be anything touching it directly except this." He tapped the stone immediately behind it. "If we can shift it without disturbing anything else, we can shift the remainder one after the other."

Carrick considered the pattern of the stones. "I'd thought here." He stooped down and touched a different stone.

"Then you'd have to shift this first, and you can't be sure what's over that corner."

"Checkmate!"

"It *is* a bit like chess," conceded Prentice.

They were still arguing when the others arrived. The argument broadened. After a little there were five separate views.

Carrick looked at his watch. "Everybody here?"

"Except Witton."

"He said he might be walking over from Milking Gap."

"Let's begin then! We'll move your stone." Carrick nodded at Prentice.

Prentice went back to the tool hut and put his plate inside.

"I think if you eased it an inch this way first . . ." Carrick looked up abstractedly. "I almost forgot—we can expect to be attacked some time this morning." He looked at the shocked incredulity on Miss Kirton's face, chuckled, and said soothingly, "By three children. They're infiltrating across the Wall. Give me a shout if you see any sign of them." He crouched down. "Two of you work your fingers underneath and see if you can shift it toward me."

Patiently the work began. The stone stayed trapped. They cleared earth very gently, very gingerly from its farther end. A fragment of pottery was jammed tightly against it.

They freed that, and the block gave and stuck again. Once more they worked at the earth beyond the farther face.

Miss Kirton, handling the shard of pottery, said, "A piece of a lamp. We might find the rest of it."

They moved the stone half an inch. It stuck again, and they moved it back.

Carrick squatted on his heels staring at it. "Would it come straight up now?"

"Not a hope." Prentice pointed to where the adjoining stone overhung it slightly.

It was clearly going to be a long job. The others drifted away to their own work. Carrick, Prentice, and one other man wrestled with the stone. Miss Kirton supervised.

Prentice caught his finger against a sharp fragment of rock and muttered like an angry badger.

The other man worried: "If we could get a lever to it..."

"It'll come," said Carrick placidly. "There's plenty of time."

They moved the stone back again its permitted half inch. Earth fell between it and the side and had to be cleared out with a brush. They began all over again, careful, patient, methodical.

Miss Kirton sketched the plan of the stones in relation to the dish with meticulous care, measuring from point to point with a steel tape. Finally, she fetched a paint pot and a small brush and numbered them away from the edge of the dish.

Prentice immediately smudged his thumb over a number and said, "Blast!"

Miss Kirton grinned wickedly at him.

The stone came clear suddenly for no specific reason that anyone could see. They lifted it and carried it awkwardly away from the excavated section—it weighed perhaps thirty pounds—positioned it on the turf and came back.

Miss Kirton was down in the excavation, peering at the newly exposed face of earth. "Three quarters of an inch of ash and cinders—wind-blown, at a guess; there hasn't been any fire here. After that it's just earth—earth and grass roots. The rest of the lamp is there. We'll get it out when Pettit gets over as far as this. There's something else beyond, a different kind of ware. I can't tell now."

She straightened herself from the hole, and the four of them gathered round the next block of stone, their foreheads wrinkled as they tried to solve the problems it presented.

8

Mig watched the tiny bird with one eye. It was barely fifteen inches from her nose. It sat quite motionless except for minute movements of its head, and its own beady eye stared back at hers. She felt almost that "glared" would have been the better word, if one could talk of a wren glaring. It was quite apparent that it regarded her with disfavor.

She wanted to look at her watch, but that was obviously impossible. She tried to squint at the sun, but to make an accurate judgment of its height she would have had to move her head, and she felt that the bird might be really angry if she did that. She winked at it instead. It put its head over on the other side and regarded her even more balefully.

Clinton rescued her. He moved suddenly and grunted, and the wren shot up in an indignant puff of brown feathers, uttered one shrill, belligerent note, impossibly loud for so tiny a body, and was gone.

Mig sat up, parted the stems of the stunted bushes, looked out, saw that the day was well into the morning, and began to sort out her thoughts. When the bird first woke her, she had had difficulty in remembering where she was. Now she was having difficulty in remembering quite how she had got there.

She said softly, "You awake, Peter?"

There was no answer. She looked across the bowl of the tiny quarry. She could see his outline between the stones and the long grass. Clinton was below her, three feet down the slope. It hadn't, she remembered, been particularly comfortable. Now that she was really awake she could feel that she was stiff all down one side, and she was sure that there was a bruise on her hip. Her feet were sore. It was all quite different from the smooth turf on which they had pitched camp at sunset.

Or *was* it last sunset? She wasn't quite certain of anything at the moment. She yawned and made another attempt to get her mind clear. Then everything seemed to click into place. Peter's plan had worked. She knew where they were now, just under the Wall itself, at the point where the stone dyke ran up from the valley bottom below Cuddy's Crags. Peter had said that he could find it in the moonlight, and he'd found it. They'd got very wet once, and she'd fallen three times—that would account for the bruise on her hip. But they'd found it.

She yawned again and wondered if she could settle down for another quarter of an hour. How much sleep had she had? Moonrise was about eleven o'clock, as far as they'd been able to remember. Clinton had set his wristwatch alarm for two hours later—that would be one o'clock—to give the moon a chance to get up over the hills. They'd packed everything except the tent rolls before they went to bed. It hadn't taken them long to get stowed in the moonlight.

Peter had the whole plan in his mind. He'd carried the torch, but they hadn't had to use it. They had had the edge of the trees in the Greenlee plantation as a guide for the first part, keeping wide of it so as not to get too close to Greenlee Farm. Then they crossed the farm road, and that was plain enough in the moonlight. They went due south after that until they could see the water of Greenlee Lough and headed for the trees at the west end of the lough. That was when they got wet; Peter had said that they probably would, and they did. And she'd fallen as they crossed the Caw Burn. She wondered how Peter remembered that it *was* the Caw Burn, but of course he'd been sitting over the map for a week.

Then they'd followed the tree edge until the trees of the lough and the Bonnyrigg trees met, and Peter had tried to find a way through and couldn't and he'd got scratched. And then they'd found the path, quite by accident, and Peter'd said that there wasn't a path marked on the map and had seemed quite annoyed about it, but Clint had said that he was just plumb thankful. They'd still had to climb over a wall to get clear of it, but they hadn't woken the dogs at Bonnyrigg Hall.

She didn't remember much after that—just walking. She could remember the shape of Peter's pack, that was about all, and she remembered following the pack in the moonlight and a few stars, and very little more, except that the ground seemed to get steeper and steeper. And when they rested, she'd gone straight off to sleep, lying back against her pack, and when Peter had woken her, he'd been almost apologetic —apologetic for Peter, that is. And then the ground was level again for a bit and soft underfoot but not soggy. She remembered that quite clearly. It wasn't soggy because of the dry weather, but she was sure that they'd been walking over a bog. And then she could remember the ground quite black and very steep in the moon shadow, and she'd known that it was the Great Whin Sill, and she hadn't cared. She was past caring about anything by then.

Finally they'd reached the stone dyke just beyond the old limekiln, and they'd been too tired to climb over it. But Peter kept saying that they had to get on the other side, and she remembered Clint asking if it was the Wall, and she'd said "Stoopid!" and he'd snapped at her, and in another ten paces they'd forgotten what it was about.

She really didn't remember anything at all after that except something about scrambling over a gap and Peter saying, "We've done it! And there's enough scrub to cover us. I knew there would be! I knew there would be!" But she couldn't remember where they'd been when he'd said it. Here perhaps.

She parted the bushes for a second time and looked up the steepest part of the slope. Across the skyline there were three courses of careful, regular stonework, and she said, surprised even inside her own mind, "It's the Wall! It really *is* the Wall!"

She couldn't wait any longer. She leaned over on her elbow, stretched out her arm, and pinched Peter's foot. He was blearily awake at once. She said, "Sun's a-scorching your eyes out. It's ten to nine."

He sat up. "We made it!" he exclaimed wonderingly.

Mig said, "You can see the Wall. Look through the bushes! Careful!"

He peered out as she had done. When he spoke again, his voice was awed. "I think I was half asleep when we came up here," he admitted honestly.

"I was fast asleep," said his sister. "I don't remember a thing except your saying that we'd done it. Shall I wake Clint?" She wriggled down the slope, bent double, and got hold of Clinton's ear. "Wakey! Wakey!"

Clinton groaned, stretched himself, and said, "Where am I? Don't tell me! I don't even care."

They sorted themselves out of the bedding with enormous difficulty. The scrub was surprisingly high, but it would not do more than cover them sitting bolt upright. Still with great difficulty, they rolled the bedding and strapped it on the packs. They ate cheese between biscuits and drank water. There was no question of coffee.

"Smell would give us away for half a mile," said Peter with authority.

They put on dry stockings. Their shoes were still wet, but Mig described hers hopefully as "dampish." With the last of the water from the bottle they washed the sleep out of their eyes. Finally they stacked the three packs together under the thickest of the bushes.

They were doing this when Mig heard the falling stone. All three froze instantly. They were drilled to this now. There was another little scatter of falling fragments. They heard a heavy boot sgurr on stone above their heads.

Peter peered cautiously through the tops. Mig had found her own peephole. They saw the man's head simultaneously. He was hatless, and he carried a sports jacket slung over his shoulder rather like a cloak. He walked a little hunched, his head down. He had a thin beard. From where they crouched, he looked angry. From the head of the gully at the point at which Mig had spotted the ashlar of the Wall, he came into full view. He was tall, thin, and either tired or angry or both. As he stared up the slope beyond the gully, he kicked at something crossly, and there was another scatter of small stones, and then a single larger stone bounding down the steep.

"Stinker!" said Mig belligerently.

"Sssh! It's our chance." For a moment Peter waited, staring fixedly at the rounded shoulders going up the slope. Then he said, "Quick!" He moved out of the scrub soundlessly and ran crouched to the head of the gully with Mig at his heels and Clinton barely three yards behind.

As she ran, Mig tried to watch the sweep second hand of Peter's watch—she was to do the timekeeping.

Above them the man went on, his body beginning to shorten now as the slope hid him.

Peter said nothing. They'd agreed exactly what they meant to do. A buttress of rock covered them at last completely. When they came to the brief flat space at the base of the Wall, there was no sign of the man.

Mig said, breathing hard, "Forty-three."

Peter swung an imaginary grapnel.

Mig began to count. "One, two, three—go!"

Peter found a foothold and scrambled up the Wall. It was a fraction over six feet here. He made no effort to hurry; he still had twenty-seven seconds.

Mig said, "Over!" and to Clinton, "Up you go!"

Clinton moved slowly, waiting for the word that marked his allowed thirty seconds. She gave it to him and started up herself.

Peter was across the Wall and down already on the other side. As he moved crouched across it, he saw out of the corner of his eye the head and shoulders of the man on the crest. He was still moving steadily ahead, not looking round. Below him Peter saw a deep patch of fern at the base of a spur of rock. Beyond that were rushes and another stunted rowan. He made first for the fern, looked up, could see no sign of the man, and passed to the rushes. Behind him he could see Clinton running doubled up. He didn't bother about Mig; he knew she would be there. Barely half a minute later they were all lying panting in the cover of the bracken.

Mig said triumphantly, "Two minutes forty-three seconds! Even allowing for Clint jumping the gun by two seconds, that's not bad."

"He never turned," said Peter, "nor would the Wall patrol. Nobody would, going up a slope like that with a friend behind him on the other side. I knew he wouldn't."

"And now?"

"The digging's just down below us somewhere. We'll see how near we can get to it before we're spotted. You watch that side, Clint! I'll lead. Mig, you watch this side!"

Mig had got her breath back. "Where d'you think he was going?"

"Housesteads," replied her brother. "Come on!"

They moved cautiously through the gully. It widened out on to the broad slope below the grassy track that marked the Military Way.

Mig stopped them when they had gone thirty yards. "There he is!"

The man was going down the grass slope with enormous strides. Ahead of him they could see the roof of a small wooden shed and a foot or two of the sides. Beyond the ridge they could see a gathering of heads and shoulders.

"That'll be the dig. Back a bit!" Peter ordered.

They retreated into the shelter of the hollow.

The man strode down the last of the slope and joined the heads beyond.

Peter said, "He must be one of the Prof's men. I wonder if he was watching for us."

All three began to laugh. When they were quiet again, Peter gave them the plan. "We'll keep over to the right for a bit. Stay in the hollow. Then we'll use the shelter of the ridge and try to get behind the shed. If we can do that, we can rush the dig."

"Injun fightin'!" Clinton was scornful. He tapped his mouth in an almost silent war cry.

"This *was* the wild frontier," said Mig.

They laughed again, filled with triumphant excitement.

Once, almost at the summit of the ridge, they had to lie with hardly more than the tussocks of grass for cover while one of the girls came to the shed for a tray. As she went back, they heard a voice call out, and people climbed from other parts of the digging and moved to where the Professor stood. The girl with the tray followed them.

"Quick!" said Peter as the group came together.

The three ran openly now. In a moment the shed covered them. They reached it and passed to the far end.

"Mig, nip over and stand next to the Prof and see what happens!"

They watched her as she moved swiftly and silently across the turf. She was standing beside Dr. Carrick for a full half minute before he noticed her. Even then he was abstracted. They saw Mig lift one hand and heard the war cry, ending with the triumphant: "Yet! Yet! Yet!"

The bent shoulders clustered round the excavation straightened with quick, startled movements. Heads turned round. Two of the younger men leaped to their feet.

As the boys crossed the intervening space, they heard the Professor answering Mig's triumph. "Up wi' Tarret and Tarset Burn! Down with the Rede and the Tyne!"

Miss Kirton looked up indignantly. "What on earth . . . ?"

The Professor disregarded her. "I take it I've lost my bet, but I can't pass your battle cry. You're fifteen hundred years out. Tell your father he's been mixing his periods again."

"How did you know it was Dad?" demanded Mig.

Carrick scratched his chin. "I know his style." The boys had reached them. Carrick looked at them over the top of his spectacles. "Nobody saw you?"

Peter nodded. "Nobody. We had a terrific time getting past the fire watchers on the Bell Crags yesterday, but we did it."

"And you came straight over the Wall?"

"No, sir. We waited until we heard somebody on it. We let him pass just as they would have let the sentries separate, and then we slipped over behind him."

"He didn't turn round?"

"No, sir."

"Sure he didn't see you?"

"Ask him," said Peter, playing his ace of trumps.

"Who?"

Mig moved quickly over until she was close to Witton. "The Roman sentry." She lifted up one hand in a Roman salute.

The young man with the beard looked furious. The rest of the team laughed, some of them unkindly. Witton was not terribly popular.

"Did you see anything, Witton?" demanded the Professor.

Witton hesitated for a second before he said reluctantly, "No."

"Hear anything?" Carrick was remorseless.

"No." He scowled at the two boys and there was another general laugh. "I wasn't expecting . . ." he began in self-defense.

Carrick nodded. "You weren't here when I warned the rest."

Mig put her hands into the pockets of her shorts. "He was walking like this." She hunched her shoulders and lowered her chin. "You looked frightfully cross."

Again there was a general laugh.

Underneath it she caught Witton's voice. "Infernal kids!"

9

"Right!" said the Professor. "Back to work."

Mig came over to him. "What's happening?"

"We're trying to move the second block . . ." Carrick checked himself. "Of course you don't know! I told your father, but you haven't seen him since." He paused for a moment before he asked, "D'you know the great Mildenhall dish?"

Peter said, "Dad took us to see it time before last when we were in London."

Mig nodded. "It's wonderful. You haven't . . .?"

Carrick made a quick gesture with his hand. "We've found something like it, I think. It's pinned between big blocks of ashlar, and we've got to move the stones one by one till we get to it."

Peter asked wonderingly, "Like the Mildenhall treasure?"

"We don't know—yet." Carrick's voice was completely honest. "We know it's good. It's a huge silver platter. We don't know anything else."

Clinton said almost plaintively, "Explain!"

Carrick looked down at him. "We haven't met."

"Clinton Hammond." Peter rushed in hastily with the introduction. "He's staying with us. He's American."

Carrick nodded. "How do you do? These two know me. They don't need explanations. The Mildenhall treasure was discovered when a field in Suffolk was deep ploughed in the war. They found a quantity of Roman silver." He looked up with a gentle smile that was almost of derision at himself. "Quantity of Roman silver be hanged! They found the finest treasure that's ever been discovered in Britain. Nothing like it anywhere else. Miraculous stuff! Wait a minute!" He crouched down. "Not that way up! Move it to the left first. Even half an inch will give you clearance."

The three crouched down with him, absorbed.

Miss Kirton said, "There's a fragment of glass at the top corner. There may be more. Don't splinter it!"

Prentice said suddenly, "Right! Lift now!"

The block came up with perfect ease, as if there had been no problem about it at all, as if there had never been any question of its jamming. In the impress of the position where it had lain there was a tiny glass vase shattered into perhaps a hundred fragments. Miss Kirton crooned over it. Three of the men carried the block out and placed it next to the first one. The drawing board was brought, and the position of the vase marked carefully upon it.

Prentice said, "No fire here. A little ash drifted down between the blocks; that's all."

One of the girls began to work with a brush against the base of the next block.

Miss Kirton filled the bottom of a tin box with plasticine and began to lift the fragments of the vase out one by one with a pair of forceps and to plant them in careful order on the soft base.

Carrick took the three down the length of the building, showing them where the fire had scarred the stone and where charcoal and ash showed that it had consumed the contents of the western half. "It wasn't a temple," he said in answer to a direct question of Mig's. "It was too small for an ordinary dwelling house for anybody who could afford the sort of things that we are finding. If the Romans had developed the English weekend habit, I'd call it a weekend cottage. Maybe we'll find something that will help us before we're finished. It's a puzzle."

"Dad says archaeology's mostly working out puzzles," said Peter solemnly.

Carrick laughed. "He's about right. The trouble is that most of the puzzles have about three different answers. Does it all seem a lot of nonsense to you, Clinton?"

"No, *sir!* I'm beginning to see what it means."

Carrick laughed again. "It's about the only thing left that you can't put through a computer."

Mig asked diffidently, "Are you going to let us see the dish?"

"Good heavens! I forgot that you hadn't even seen it. Come along!"

Carrick took them back to the point where the little crowd had been gathered at the start. Miss Kirton abandoned her vase. He showed them the top edge and the back of the great silver disk. "We don't know what the edge pattern is. We know that it has a slightly raised foot, and we know that there are scratches inside the foot."

Miss Kirton said, "And we know that there are raised figures across the dish itself. Give me your hand, Mig!"

Mig, looking faintly surprised, held out her right hand.

Miss Kirton put her fingers round the slender wrist. Then she turned Mig's hand palm upward and examined the tips of her fingers. Finally she looked up at Carrick, nodded, and turned back to Mig. "Can you feel things?"

Peter answered first. "She can. She can tell anything with her fingers."

Mig said more doubtfully, "Yes, I think so."

"With that wrist," said Miss Kirton, "she could get her hand inside. Can she try?"

"Try, but don't strain it, Mig. We don't know how strong the metal is." Carrick grinned at Clinton. "All archaeologists are impatient. The whole business of being a professor is to restrain natural impatience."

Miss Kirton said, "Huh!" inelegantly, and then to Mig, "Get on to the far stone, child!" She wiped Mig's slightly grubby fingers with her handkerchief. "Settle yourself comfortably and then slide your hand in here." She put her finger on the circumference of the dish at the point where it was farthest away from the stone.

Mig closed her fingers, flattened her hand, and slid it in. It jammed almost at once. She withdrew it and tried again a little farther along. Again it jammed. The fleshy part at the base of her palm caught on the edge of the dish and bulged.

Miss Kirton called out surprisingly, "Butter!" and then in explanation, "Get me some butter from the lunch packets!" Carrick watched, amused. When it came, she oiled Mig's palm and the back of her hand. "Try another half inch along!"

Carrick said, "Not entirely scientific." And Miss Kirton looked up malevolently.

Mig wriggled her hand, found a place that seemed easy, and stretching out her thumb wide to reduce the thickness of the flesh, delicately slipped her whole hand through the slit.

"Splendid!" exclaimed Miss Kirton. "Splendid! What can you feel?"

Mig was quite silent. When Peter looked at her, he saw that her eyes were shut. They could see faint movement in her wrist as her hand moved, apparently almost independent of it, in the darkness between the silver and the stone.

"What do you feel?" asked Miss Kirton again.

"Wait!" Professor Carrick stopped her, watching the child's face.

Mig was smiling faintly. They could see the tiny movement going on and on. One of the other girls came up and watched, then Prentice. Somebody else followed him. A feeling that something was about to happen spread right through the digging. There was complete silence.

Then Mig said softly, "It's perfect! It's beautiful, so beautiful!"

Miss Kirton looked up at Carrick and the Professor nodded. "What is so beautiful?" she asked, very gently.

"It's a girl," said Mig. "She's holding up her hands." She extended her left arm above her head suddenly, sketching in with an extraordinary realism a graceful line. "And there's something coming down to her fingers—birds, I think—yes, birds—a flight of them." She indicated wings with her forefinger. "She's dancing with birds, I think. Gulls, it could be—and other birds." She was silent again.

Peter murmured, his voice hardly above a whisper, "She can tell the pattern on the back of a foreign coin with her eyes shut."

"She's got nothing on," said Mig, "except a veil or something, and it's swirling up—in the wind, I think."

"What is she standing on?"

"I can't reach it," Mig answered. "I can only reach as far as her knees. There's something to the left, something curling. It could be spray on a wave perhaps. I don't know. There's nothing at all that I can feel to the left of her, but there's something to the right."

Again they watched the curious movement of her wrist as she strained the tips of her fingers to the extreme limit of her reach.

"There's another figure there. I can't make out what it

is. I think it's an elbow. I'm sorry. I can't tell you anything more about it. It could be a veil—or a bent branch even. Wait a bit! There are birds above it too—high above it and small." Her fingers went back to the central figure. "She's lovely!" Her voice dropped a little. "Lovely."

Carrick said, "You'd better get your wrist out, Mig, before the flow of blood ceases entirely. I think a young girl should be attached to every dig in future."

Miss Kirton looked up at her. "Thank you. I can't tell you how much!"

Mig pulled at the flesh of her arm until her hand slid away. Her wrist came out, and she sat rubbing it gently between her finger and her thumb. "It's the most beautiful thing I've ever touched," she said soberly.

"The least we can do," said Carrick, "is to offer you the best lunch that we can scratch up, and it won't be a banquet at that. Where did you leave your packs?"

"Far side of the Wall," replied Peter. "We reckoned we'd make the last dash light."

"As a matter of interest, what would you have done if you *had* been barbarians from the north?"

Peter considered carefully for a moment. "Burned this maybe."

"Or cut straight down into the valley," suggested Mig. "The vallum wouldn't have stopped us."

"Never stopped anybody," said a voice from the crowd.

Carrick fixed Clinton with his eye. "What would you have done?"

The American boy thought carefully. "I don't see that a party of three or four'd do a lot of good trying to beat up a place as thick as this must have been with Roman G.I.'s. I reckon we'd be aimin' for a point in the valley and pretty set on gettin' there."

"Would you have burned this house as you ran?"

Clinton considered the problem. "Pretty temptin'," he said at last.

"Guesswork!" Witton, sitting at the back of the little crowd, was full of scorn.

"Somebody burned it," said the Professor slowly—"burned it and didn't stay to loot. It might have been a single raid; it might have happened when they came over the Wall in Valens' time. The dish is fourth century beyond a doubt from what Mig told us."

"More guesswork!" Witton buried his face in his mug of coffee.

"We'll know by tomorrow." Carrick smiled at Mig to cover the rudeness. "What do you want as a reward?"

Mig put her head on one side and grinned at him, completely disregarding Witton. "How much did you bet against us?"

Carrick grunted as everybody laughed.

"We'll get it out of Dad anyway," said Mig sedately, "but it would help us if we knew how much."

Even Witton joined in the laughter at this.

When it died, Carrick said reluctantly, "A fiver."

Soberly Peter nodded. "He must have been pretty confident about us."

"He was," admitted Carrick candidly. "That's why I went so high! Come on! Back to work!"

Mig looked at her watch surreptitiously. After a few minutes she drifted away up the slope. There was no real cover, but when she calculated that she was out of earshot, she settled and slipped out the transistor set. It lacked still three minutes to twelve. She ignored the end of a dull talk. When it was over, she turned the little milled wheel to bring up the volume. Her thumb slipped, and the signature tune of the Mosspickers blared out across the noonday silence.

Down at the diggings Carrick's head lifted like a startled stag's. "What in the name of Orpheus. . . ?"

"Mig," said Clinton. "She *has* to listen to the Mosspickers at twelve o'clock, or she goes off her eats."

Carrick looked at him ferociously. "Now I *know* you're barbarians from the north!"

10

In the middle of the afternoon they lifted the third stone. That left two more.

Clinton, lying on his stomach in the sun and picking his teeth with a stalk of grass, said, "Why don't they get with it? I got psychological problems. They could shift the other two inside half an hour."

Mig shook her head. "They could have had it out two days ago if it comes to that, but they've got to see how the layers lie, the stuff that's filled in above it. They've got to try to find something that they can put a date to and that was buried at the same time."

"What's it matter?"

"Everything—to them. Dad says archaeologists dig to . . ." She paused a moment to consider the appropriate words, remembered what her father had said, and quoted, ". . . infuriate other archaeologists."

Carrick, sitting near by, overheard her and chuckled. "Proof—we've got to have proof. Nobody believes us otherwise. Wait till the newspapers get on to this, and the reporters come down on us like hawks!"

It was Mig's turn to chuckle.

Prentice called them, and they went down to help him

shift sifted earth. On the third journey with the wheel-barrow Peter missed his footing and fell into a trench. Clinton saved the barrow.

From the far end of the trench they heard Witton's grumbling voice. "Haven't you kids messed up things enough for one day?"

Peter said, "Sorry. I slipped."

"Old enough to be careful in a place like this," said Witton, without turning round.

Clinton pointed five fingers at him—his father had had a spell of duty in Greece. Witton, however, missed the gesture, and they moved, giggling, with the barrow to Prentice at the spoil dump.

Peter jerked his head back. "Why's he so mad?"

"He gets that way sometimes," replied Prentice. "Don't take any notice."

Mig giggled. "Perhaps he's been crossed in love."

"I'll ask him if you like," Prentice offered.

"Heavens, no! It's bad enough as it is."

They worked on through the long afternoon, immensely happy to be called on for anything. The American boy was fascinated by the care and the patience, and perhaps by the solemnity of it all. Only Carrick himself, and sometimes Prentice, seemed prepared to be frivolous. It was hot and at times drowsily quiet. Mig stole half an hour of sleep at one point, stretched out behind a pile of stones. From time to time men knocked off for a smoke or a rest. Miss Kirton herself went away for half an hour. But Carrick kept alive through every moment, watching, the children declared afterwards, every handful of earth lifted and sifted and searched.

By five o'clock the plan of the building had been advanced materially. Carrick was certain now that the dish had been in the end room of the eastern part of the building, that there had been three rooms in all with light partitions, rather than honest walls, between them. Just before five o'clock Prentice discovered the first few tesserae of a mosaic pavement. By half past five they had cleared enough earth to be sure that it was a simple pattern of alternate lines of black and white.

When they were clear on that point, Carrick said, "Right! We'll call it a day."

Miss Kirton asked for another ten minutes and was told to "pack it up." Her glass vase was already safe.

The day's finds were wrapped and taken down to Carrick's car. When the routine was all complete, Carrick said, "What about you three? Shall I give you a lift?"

Peter shook his head. "We phone Dad at eight o'clock. He'll pick us up."

"Where will you phone him from?"

"The Twice Brewed." Peter named the new pub that was called after the ancient carters' inn. "Dad said we were to make love to Mrs. Radlett and get her to give us something to eat while we wait for him."

"What are you going to do until eight o'clock?"

"Go over the Wall to the Greenlee Lough and have a swim."

Carrick nodded approvingly. "Wouldn't mind it myself. It's hot."

"We've got to pick up our gear anyway," Peter explained.

"Head for the gap where the Jenkins Burn runs into the loff." The Professor pronounced the word Northumberland fashion. "You'll see a bit of a path running to the east. It looks bad but it isn't. There's a beach at the end of it ten feet square. It's enough for bathing. I'm not going to start thanking you about today"—he looked at Mig and then at the others—"but if there's anything I can do . . ."

Mig said at once, "Can we come tomorrow and be here when you free the dish?"

Carrick smiled at them. "You've earned it. Of course you can! Square it with your father and tell him I said I'd be glad to have you."

They waited while the different parties moved off.

Blake had the guard duty for the night. He was a middle-aged man. Neither Peter nor Mig had met him before. He had been working all day at the far end of the dig, and they scarcely knew him, but they stayed chatting with him after the last carload had gone. Only Witton was left.

He came up to where they were talking with Blake and asked pointedly, "When are you kids going?"

Peter shrugged his shoulders. "There's no hurry."

"There isn't supposed to be anybody on the site after the Prof has gone," said Witton rudely.

Peter looked at Blake. The older man's face was expressionless, but it seemed clear that he resented the other's tone.

Mig said, "Oh, all right! Come on—let's go!" And glared at Witton.

Peter said politely, "Good-bye, Mr. Blake."

They strolled up the hill, moving easily.

Mig said, very clearly and very distinctly, "Stinker!" Her voice was pitched to carry just as far as the dig.

Automatically Peter muttered, "Shut up, Mig!" But his tone had no conviction.

They walked in silence for a minute or two, and then Clinton said, "Titanium-plated stinker!"

For no particular reason they broke into a run, scurrying up the hill giggling. For no particular reason Peter led them up the steep instead of following the lower slope to the notch. In a minute they could see the Wall. Just before the summit they stopped to breathe.

Mig turned back and looked down the long, rolling slope

to the Tyne valley. The late sun had brought out shadows and colors that had not been there in the morning. The shapes were altered. It was as if some great sculptor had carved the whole landscape afresh. Only the mountains of the Lake District over to the southwest still kept their contours. There were more people about now, more cars on the road below, more dots going up and coming down from the slope that led to Housesteads. The National Trust car park was full. On the sector of the Wall between them and the Housesteads wood they could see a dozen people. She wheeled round to see if she could yet see the Wall to the west. There were two youths standing on the skyline. Her eyes swept along the shoulder of the ridge. A third of the way down there were three men, one of them sprawled on his back apparently fast asleep. The second was turned away from her. The third was sitting up. He had a pair of binoculars to his eyes.

She said, "I wonder how long *they*'ve been there."

"Who?"

"Those three men." She pointed them out to Peter.

"Just taking a rest. The Wall's steep along the ridge."

"If they were there when we came through"—Mig indicated with a single finger the gully that they had used to cover their approach to the digging—"they'd have seen us."

"That was hours ago!"

"What's he peekin' at?" demanded Clinton.

"Bird watchers," said Peter scornfully.

"In town clothes?" asked Mig.

They began to climb again over the last few feet to the summit.

Mig said, "If they were there this morning, they saw us. I think we've got to tell Dad."

"He'll say, 'Sitting there all day in those hot clothes'!"

"What did they do about a drink?" Mig imitated her father faithfully.

They reached the summit and stopped to look forward at the other view—the view across the country over which they had come so blindly in the night.

"Hip flask!" said Clinton quietly.

"Hip what? Oh, I see! The drinks business. Could be."

They forgot about the men and walked forward, trying to pick out the fire watchers' tower as they went. They were on the Wall itself before they spotted it, and they turned and moved carefully down the slope to the point where they had crossed. When they reached it, they dropped off and went down till they were level with the sleeping place.

"Do we take our gear?" asked Peter.

"We do not!" said Mig lazily. "You wouldn't let us bring swimsuits. There's nothing we need."

"Map—I don't know where this Jenkins Burn is."

"All right! We can use it now," said Mig.

They waited while Peter undid his rucksack, pulled out the Ordnance Survey map and consulted it gravely.

"Straight down the stone dyke to the limekiln," he said, "and veer left a bit at the end of it."

Twenty-five minutes later they were at the edge of the lough. It stretched ahead of them, placid, intensely blue. There was no slightest sign of man anywhere.

Clinton said, "I'm learnin' about England."

"Such as . . . ?"

"I thought it was all tame."

"Not in the Border country, kookie," said Mig promptly. "It never was, and it never will be."

They found the Professor's path. As he had said, it looked unpromising, but they followed it under the steep of the hill. It ran round a little promontory, all but disappeared, recovered, ran round another miniature point, and took them straight to the Professor's beach. It was as small as he had promised.

Mig walked sedately to the farther end of it. "Girls' dressing room!" she called, and began to strip down to her underthings.

The boys turned and slipped off their shorts and shirts. Within a minute they were floating in the deep amber water, Mig with her eyes shut and her hands paddling just enough to keep her horizontal. The sweat and the heat of the sun washed off them. The place was wholly peaceful. Secret.

It seemed a long time after that that Clinton asked, "Who owns this pool?"

"Pool nothing!" retorted Mig indignantly. "It's a loff. Add that to your list of English pronunciations, you ignorant Yankee!"

"Ah'm from de Souf ma self," said Clinton lazily, "but I wouldn't expect the English to be able to differentiate. Who *does* it belong to?"

"Bonnyrigg Hall," said Peter, "or West Hotbank Farm —I wouldn't know. Why?"

"I think"—Clinton's voice was airy—"that the owner's coming to ask us about it."

Peter and Mig popped up instantly and started treading water. They could see no sign of life along the shore.

"Where?"

"This away," drawled Clinton.

Across the lough, intensely white on the blue water, its wings raised in a splendid arrogance, was a male swan. It was moving so fast that its breast feathers set up a bow wave in front of it, and the wave, oddly, was amber brown.

Mig made a queer throaty noise, and the bird's head turned instantly towards her. "Come on, Horace! I'm afraid we've nothing to give you to eat, though. We left our bags up on the Sill."

"How do you know its name is Horace?" asked Clinton reasonably.

"All swans are named Horace," explained Mig frivolously, "until you have information to the contrary."

Peter said, "Cripes!"

The bird came up slowing, decided to be friendly, and paddled between them.

"We heard you last night, Horace," said Mig. "What were you flighting around in the dark for?"

The swan hissed softly.

Mig asked vaguely of the air in front of her, "The question is: Are you hotter when you come up a steep hill after a bathe than you were before it?"

"A point," agreed the American boy.

"Get your rucksack fixed and don't talk so much!" said Peter, becoming the elder brother. "We haven't any time to spare. It's exactly two miles to The Twice Brewed, and it's twenty to eight. We're going to be late anyway."

"Will your dad be mad?"

Peter grinned. "We have a working system. If he says eight o'clock, we've got until half past. We know it, he knows it; and it's all right. He just sets the time ahead—he thinks we don't notice."

Clinton laughed. "My pop uses watch time."

They moved up the last stretch of the slope and climbed the Wall exactly where they had climbed it triumphantly in the early morning.

On the far side Peter said, "We'll strike up a bit. There's some rough ground as I remember—and nettles. Doesn't make any difference really."

He went ahead to lead. They had walked for perhaps a

hundred yards when Mig said, "Who's that coming up the slope?"

"Witton the Wet!" exclaimed Peter, his voice surprised. "I didn't see him. Lucky you spotted him, Mig!"

"What do we do?"

"Squat," replied Peter promptly. "We don't want to get involved in an argument."

Clinton nodded approvingly. "He's a jerk. Where's he headin'?"

Mig whispered—they had lowered their voices for no particular reason at all—"Somebody said he'd left his car at Milking Gap."

Peter jerked his thumb. "Along that way."

They sat on the springy green turf between stalks of the sparse bracken and waited.

After a little Peter raised himself and peered down hill. "Moving to the right." He settled down again. "He'll be round the shoulder in a minute."

Mig, lying back comfortably against her rucksack, said softly, "Stinker!"

"Square stinker!" Clinton capped it.

"Oblong, oval, rhomboidal stinker!" Mig offered the alternatives happily.

Peter waited till he judged that Witton would be out of sight and then lifted himself up again. As he did so, a hard voice called, "Over here!"

The three youngsters looked at each other.

"Now who would that be?" asked Clinton.

A voice, recognizably Witton's, called out, "Right!"

Clinton said, "The city slickers!"

"Couldn't be," said Peter. "How'd he know them?"

"That's where they were," said Mig positively. "Down the shoulder there."

"I gotta see this!" Clinton lifted himself to his feet cautiously.

"Not that way!" Peter pointed. "Up the hill and come round above them."

"Makes sense," agreed the boy.

They moved warily, keeping the line of the slope between them and the voices. Peter set a fast pace, and they were breathless when he finally sketched a sharp gesture with his hand. They came up to him and peered over. Down below them, perhaps eighty feet lower, was the little hollow where the three men had lain. They were sitting bolt upright now, and Witton was squatting on his heels facing them.

Peter whispered, "Now what the devil's all this about?"

"He's telling them somethin'."

As they watched, Witton's hand made a rounded gesture as if it ran up and down the curve of a rainbow and back again.

Mig said sharply, "He can't be telling them about the dish!"

"He can too," said Clinton sardonically.

Peter muttered, "They were all sworn to secrecy."

They were sitting back on their haunches now.

Painstakingly Mig made the gesture that Witton had made. "If you were telling somebody what to look for . . ." She stopped and looked up, scared, and her hand made the gesture again—this time faltering.

"He wouldn't." Peter shook his head vigorously.

"What's he doing yakkin' with guys like that then?"

"The voice," Mig began hesitantly, "it was a southerner's voice—didn't belong to anybody around here."

"It was educated."

"So what? They're thugs, all the three of them."

"One of them was educated at least."

"Take another peek!" Clinton insisted. "They're *thugs*."

Peter moved forward and peered over again. One of the three strangers was laying down the law. He pointed down the ridge; then he made a sweep with one hand athwart it to the north. It was clear that he was the educated southerner —they could hear the voice rise and fall, but it was impossible to make out words. One of the other men seemed to be angry. Witton was apparently defending himself. They saw him take a piece of paper out of his pocket and draw or write on it; they could not tell which. He showed it to the man with the southern voice. Then the argument started again.

Peter and the other two moved back from the edge. He looked worriedly at his watch. "We're going to be late, even if we go now."

"Go . . .?" Mig's voice was incredulous.

"We promised," said Peter.

"And leave those three gorillas?" asked Clinton.

Peter wavered. "Let's take another look."

Witton was standing up. They heard two words, the first that they had been able to make out, ". . . must go!" There was a brief argument. Then Witton climbed out of the hollow and moved fast along the slope towards Milking Gap. The three men talked, their heads close together for a long minute; then they settled down again much as they had been when Mig had spotted them in the late afternoon: one on his back, one sitting, the leader with the binoculars sweeping the country to the southwest.

"What they waitin' for?" demanded Clinton.

Mig added caustically, "The pubs are open."

"They may not be waiting for anything at all," said Peter, trying to sound reasonable. "They may be expecting somebody. That could be what they were talking to Witton about. He might have been drawing a map for them of the way somebody would come."

"And why"—Mig's voice was sharp—"would they be

waiting up here? Anybody like them would come with a car, and they'd be waiting on the Carlisle road."

"Three men like that . . ."

"Three thugs," said Clinton equably, "and they've just been talking to a jerk."

" 'Tisn't as if there were anything to steal . . ." Peter began.

"Nothing to steal!" Mig turned on him like a fury. "The dish!"

"There's a guard on the dig," said Peter hurriedly. "We know that—Mr. Blake."

"Do *they?*"

"How would they know there was anything to steal?"

"The jerk," said Clinton at once.

"But he'd have told them there was a guard."

"Mr. Blake . . ." Mig's voice was suddenly horrified.

"And *three* thugs!"

"Let's have another look."

There was no change in the positions of the men. The middle one of the three was still sitting there with his binoculars either at his eyes or just below them at the ready. They looked peaceful enough.

Peter looked at his watch again and then looked along the valley towards The Twice Brewed. "If one of us went and phoned Dad . . ."

Clinton snapped: "Half an hour! Any darn thing could happen—anythin'!"

"Dad couldn't get here for another hour," said Peter worriedly. "Wait a minute!"

Looking down at the dig, he saw Mr. Blake come out of the hut and walk along to the spoil dump. The man with the binoculars saw him at the same time. They heard the cold voice, but once more it was impossible to make out the words. The other two men sat up suddenly, and the leader passed the glasses along. They talked animatedly.

Blake dropped something at the spoil dump, turned, and went back to the shed. The three men subsided. Far to the east along the Carlisle road a car came into sight with its headlights on.

Peter led the way back to their packs, and they sat down soberly. For a moment or two they were quite silent.

Then Mig said, "It's later than we thought. They're going to wait till it's dark, wait until Mr. Blake's asleep or off his guard, and they're going to steal the dish."

"We're just imagining . . ." began Peter.

"We're not, you know," said Mig stoutly. "You're thinking just what I'm thinking."

Peter said, "They don't steal from diggings."

"They do so! What about Raeburn Foot?"

Clinton said, "Explain!"

"There was a digging near the fort at the Raeburn Foot, and somebody stole two statues—little bronze statues."

"*And* an arm purse," Mig added.

"Was Professor Carrick . . . ?"

"It wasn't his dig."

"Look!" said Mig. "It isn't any use talking. We've got to warn Mr. Blake."

"How?'

"Go down and tell him," answered Mig bluntly.

"That gang'd be after us," said Clinton, not apprehensively, simply stating a fact.

They were silent again, thinking.

Once more it was Mig who put the solution. "We'll go back the way we came—along the Wall—and head to the diggings from the Housesteads side. They won't see us till we're nearly there."

"It'll take an awful time," said Peter slowly. "Dad's going to be mad—hopping mad."

"Not when we tell him," said Mig.

11

They stacked their rucksacks at the bottom of the notch and scrambled up the steep slope that Witton had climbed in the morning as hard as they could go. Mig had been tired on the last stretch up from the Greenlee Lough, but she had forgotten about it now. They made no attempt at concealment, for they knew that the men could not see them here. At the summit they began to trot, scurrying urgently along the level. There was no one in sight anywhere, only distant lights beginning to show in the first of the dusk.

Presently Peter said, "Far enough. We turn down now."

There was a rocky outcrop to the right, and they made their way carefully across it. Beyond the rock was a patch of bracken; then they came through to the clean turf again. They began to move fast down the slope.

Clinton stopped them. "What's that automobile doin'?" Almost level with them on the Carlisle road a car had slowed down, its indicator light winking furiously for a turn to the right. "No road there that I saw."

The car began to turn. The headlights swept for a little to the right and went out abruptly. It was not yet dark enough for them to be indispensable. They dimly saw the car heave at a ditch beside the road and come on.

"Wait a minute!" Peter exclaimed. "There's an old quarry track or something. I remember seeing it from the dig. D'you think . . . ?"

"Could be," said Clinton. "Get-away car."

"Wet Witton's?"

"It came from the east." Peter was thinking fast. "He had to get to Milking Gap. No, it couldn't be his. Maybe it was that that they were arguing about. Come on! Let's move."

They plunged down the hill again. Two thirds of the way to the dig they saw with a shock of despair that they were too late. Three dark figures were suddenly apparent against the afterglow in the west, striding stooped and menacingly. They were almost up to the hut before the children saw them and stopped dead in their tracks.

Peter hesitated.

Mig asked, "What do we do?"

"Shout," said Clinton.

In the same moment there was a faint cry from the hut, and Mig put her arms round herself tightly and gasped, "Oh, help us, somebody! Help us!"

The three men came away from the hut, moving swiftly, expertly. There was no further sound at all. Everything they did was sharply outlined against the afterglow. They raced on to the digging going straight to the eastern end. One man dropped to his knees. The children could see the glow of a shaded flashlight. It was clear to them that it was shining on the position of the silver dish. It switched off, and one of the men lifted something long and slender—a crowbar from the hut, Peter thought. They worked together for a moment and then heaved. Even from where the three stood tightly in a knot they could hear the clank of metal on stone and then a grinding noise. Then the crowbar was dropped, and the three men stooped and lifted one of the great stones. Again they dived for the bar. It took them longer this time—perhaps they were working with more care. Even so, it was not more than a minute before that too was moved. They tugged at something in the ground, and as they straightened, the children saw a great black disk against the western light, and at once the men started to run down the hill. The whole thing was over in less than three minutes.

Peter exclaimed, "Mr. Blake—quick!"

They unfroze and ran for the dark bulk of the hut.

Blake was on his hands and knees on the floor. He said, his voice strangely calm, "They coshed me. I wasn't asleep." He paused and then went on reasonably, "I assure you I wasn't asleep. I was lying with my head outside the door, and they coshed me."

"We'll get help." Peter's mouth was so dry that he could hardly get the words out.

"No!" said Blake. "Follow them. Find out where they go!"

Mig put in, "They've got a car."

"Well, get its number," said the painfully reasonable voice. "Go on! Go *on!*"

They were fifty yards down the slope before Clinton said, "I guess we're being crazy." He spoke hardly above a whisper, and they stopped at once. "They coshed him, the crummy ba . . ." he said warningly, cutting off the last word. "We go blinding down the hill like this, we get coshed too. No future in *that.*"

"If we could get the number of the car . . ." Peter's voice was enormously disturbed.

"We can," answered Clinton quietly. "Can't just go up and ask for it, though. We got to think it out. Where *is* the automobile?"

"I think they brought it as far down as the vallum. I

didn't look, but I doubt if they'd have got it beyond that."

"What's the vallum?"

"A ditch with mounds on either side," explained Mig. "Nobody knows what it was for."

"Skip that! Can you find it?"

Peter said, "I think so—yes."

"Right! Mig stays here. We go on, get into the ditch short of the automobile and creep up. They'll have to switch on headlights to get clear now. We'll read it then."

"I'm coming with you," announced Mig.

"Not!" said Clinton firmly.

"I'm much too scared to stay by myself."

"All right. Keep behind us then—well behind!"

They went down the hill in the darkness, the khaki and gray of their clothes concealing them in the night, picking their way carefully. Suddenly they could hear the men. Their voices were excited, cheerful.

One of them shouted, "Give us a light, Ed!"

The driver of the car switched on his sidelights for a minute.

"Facing us," whispered Clinton. "Good! He'll have to turn first."

"Look out!" called a third voice. "There's a dirty great ditch."

Ed answered, "I know."

The voice that they had heard up the hill said coldly, "Well, turn her then, you idiot! Turn her!"

The car started up and turned with much racing of the engine. It stopped again, this time with its red rear lights almost overhanging the edge of the vallum.

The two boys had slipped over the stone dyke and were in the ditch already. The fourth man was climbing out of it. Clinton moved across like a shadow, and Peter lost sight of him.

"You haven't unlocked the trunk! Can't I trust anybody?"

Somebody put something against the side of the car with a clank, and the driver's door opened.

"I think it's this one, Cap'n." The driver's voice was anxiously apologetic. "Not sure. There's a whole bunch o' keys. Firs' time I seen 'em."

"Give them to me!"

Peter, watching for the opportunity to read the number, saw a shadow slip past the brightness of the left-hand tail-light. The other two men were scrambling into the car. Almost before he realized that the shadow was Mig, it slipped away, crept silently down the steep side of the ditch and ran. He followed, moving as silently as he could. Behind him he heard the clank of metal as the lid of the trunk jerked up into position. Then suddenly the night was full of voices roaring and cursing.

Peter had almost caught up with Mig. He heard her gasp, "I've got it! I've got it!" And they ran with their hearts pounding as if they would burst.

The cold voice cut across the shouting, "Up the ditch! Mark up the ditch! It's those three infernal children."

The other voices blanketed it. Then, far away, beyond the car, high and clear in a brief silence: "Jerks!"

"Clint!" Peter could hardly get the name out.

"Going—other way!" Mig panted.

The voice of the leader reached them, "Cut him off at the fence."

Peter said, "Slow down! They're going after Clint. Needn't run ourselves to a standstill."

"You take it for a bit." Mig held out the dark circular shape to him.

Peter almost dropped it. "It's heavy! You've been running with *that?* I didn't think . . ." They trotted on along the level bottom of the ditch. "Must be all of fifteen pounds."

Mig didn't even bother to answer—she knew. She was wheezing harshly, trying to get her wind back. For a full minute they trotted in silence. Then she gasped, "What do we do now?"

"Get up—to the road—stop a car."

"What about—Clint?"

"He'll get clear. He's tough." Peter's breath was steadying. "Head for the road too, I should think. Stop for a second—listen!" The shouting was more distant still. "Nobody following us. Clint's drawn 'em right off. Let's try for the road." He headed up the slope of the ditch.

They were five yards away from it when the headlights switched on, raking across the grassland between them and the road. They jerked up and came down again. The car was moving toward them, using its headlights like searchlights, sweeping the area.

"Back!" Peter dived for the ditch.

Mig stumbled and rolled the last part.

Peter, hampered by the dish, raced down the slope, could not check himself and ran on, perilously keeping his balance.

Mig said, "It's coming this way. What do we do?"

"Won't be able to get his lights down into the ditch." Peter spoke with a confidence that he did not really feel. "Wait till he sweeps up to the road again, and we'll climb out the other side, find some long grass, and lie in it."

The car came on, lurching and twisting, its lights sometimes stabbing up almost into the sky but always coming back to the grass. Rocks, an occasional bush, a tall plant, showed up in the brilliance as if they were luminous.

Mig and Peter hurried on, keeping up a fast pace. Peter was aware that the ditch would disappear after perhaps another fifty yards. He said nothing to Mig, waiting for the car to swing its lights up to the right toward the road again. He was ready for it when it happened.

"Up! Up! Quick!"

They left the shallow protection that still remained, searching desperately for cover, and fell into, rather than chose, a patch of grass. It was barely enough to hide them, Peter knew, but enough might be enough. They could hear the car coming on. The light came back and soared over the shallowing ditch on to the hillside beyond.

"Keep down!" he urged.

Mig said indignantly, "What in Tophet d'you think I'm doing?"

The car was almost level with them now, and they spoke in the faintest of whispers. They could see the glare of the headlights through the grass stems, checking its movement.

A voice shatteringly close to them called, "I can see the end of this damned ditch. Nothing in it."

From the car the voice of the man the driver called "Cap'n" ordered, "Go on looking!"

The other man was silent for a moment. Then they heard his voice again. "Suppose they've gone up the hill?"

"Suppose they have . . ." said the cold voice evenly. "They won't get any help there. They can't get far."

"Why not?" The other voice was suddenly emboldened.

"You saw the cliffs. Would you go over there at night?"

There was a little pause before the other man said, "Be a moon later, Cap'n."

"I'm calculating on that. They're children."

Mig grunted indignantly.

Peter whispered, "Let's try to get a bit higher. I remember some thick bracken above us, I think."

Mig didn't bother to argue—she was desperately weary—and Peter added, "They'll turn the car when they get to the level at the end of the ditch and sweep round."

They moved slowly now in spite of the sense of terror that had filled them from the moment of the attack on the hut. Their legs were like lead, the joints stiff and sore, but Peter led steadily upward and Mig followed, trusting him.

Behind them the car reached the level ground. As Peter had predicted, it began to circle; then, to his immense relief, it turned first toward the road, the headlights sweeping over the uneven ground. On the line of the bank at the edge of the ditch it paused for a minute as if the driver had spotted something in the distance.

Almost as it paused, Peter panted, "The bracken!" And they found a space between the clumps and lay down wheezing, the great dish between them.

The car lights swept across the ditch and lit up the slopes beyond. It came round low down, seeming to search every tussock of grass.

Peter said thankfully, "Can't reach as high as us."

A moment later the car moved forward, cleverly using the south mound of the vallum. The lights swept up staggeringly and completed a sweep of perhaps two hundred yards before they fell away again. The car backed and prepared to use the mound once more. This time the lights flooded over them. The pair lay still, resolutely confident that they were invisible. The car pulled off the mound and trained up along the ditch again.

Peter, quite certain that they could not have been seen, lifted his head above the bracken. The other two men were coming along the edge of the ditch. They shouted to the car—it was difficult to make out the words, but it was clear that Clinton had given them the slip. The other men's voices were angry and humiliated, the voice of the Captain colder than ever. The car was still just below and a little to the left of them.

Peter said, "We've got to get out of here. They'll argue for a bit." He picked up the dish, and they moved diagonally to the northeast.

"Where are we going?" asked Mig.

"Mile-castle 37," said Peter softly. "There's broken ground round it. It'll do for a start."

"Are we going over the Wall?"

"If we have to."

Behind them the wrangle developed wonderfully. In the middle of it they heard clearly the words, "I say we should pack it in 'n scarper."

"That dish is worth thirty thousand pounds." The voice of the Captain was chillingly reasonable. "Let them get *away* with thirty thousand pounds?"

"Sooner 'n see myself in the nick," said one of the other men sullenly.

The Captain checked the argument. He said, almost quietly, "Pack it up! Get that headlight free!"

"Hurry!" urged Peter. "I hadn't thought of that. They're going to take off one of the headlights and sweep the whole slope with it."

They began to run again, the tiredness suddenly vanishing.

12

Manson asked: "The Twice Brewed? Sorry to bother you, but have three youngsters shown up during the evening?"

The woman's voice answered, "No youngsters. Two, three, couples in cars."

"No," said Manson carefully, "hiking. Boy of fifteen, girl of thirteen, 'nother boy, American, about fourteen."

"Nay, I've not seen 'em, sir."

"I told them to ask if they could use your phone and to get Mrs. Radlett to give them something to eat."

"Mrs. Radlett's no' in, sir." The woman's voice was faintly apologetic.

Manson muttered beneath his breath, "Damn!"

And the woman's voice said, "Pardon?"

"No, nothing. I was just trying to find out where they'd got to. When they do come in, keep them there, will you, please. I'll be up in half an hour."

"Sh'll they phone you?"

"They can phone my office." He gave the number. "I'm leaving now."

He put his head into his assistant's room. "My wretched children have let me down," he said mildly.

"They wouldn't do that!" Miss Graham was defensive.

"Oh, wouldn't they!" Manson growled like a bear.

"Not without good reason."

"Oh, there'll be a good reason!" Manson nodded sarcastically. "There's always a good reason. My entire family life is studded with good reasons. I'm going now. When they ring 'up, tell them I'm furious."

"I'll do that," said the girl cheerfully.

The bird called again, a quick double cry: "Kew-ick!"

Mig whispered, "Nightjar."

Peter took no notice. He was peering down into the darkness below. The voices had stopped, but occasionally the light of a powerful torch flashed out and swept a piece of ground. There were two men working up into the gully. The big question was, Where were the other two?

The bird called again, the second half of the note slightly flattened this time.

Mig said positively, "*Not* a nightjar."

Peter, his voice irritable, muttered, "For heaven's sake shut up about birds!"

"It's not a bird," replied Mig calmly. "It's Clint. He did it like that last night when he was trying to copy me." Clearly and as loudly as she dared, she answerd the call.

Instantly there was a response, still with the flattened second note.

She waited a little and answered it again.

"It's a nightjar," said Peter doubtfully.

"It isn't, you know."

Two minutes later they heard an incautious foot against a stone.

She called softly, "Here, Clint!"

The boy rose up out of the darkness. "Both of you?" he asked anxiously.

"Both of us. You all right?"

"Sure. What happened?"

"They aren't so clever," said Mig. "They put it up against the car while they opened the trunk, and I got it."

"You *got* it?" The whisper diminished into a faint whistle of admiration.

Mig tapped the dish with one knuckle, and it gave out a soft mellow sound.

"I knew you'd gone past me," said Clinton, "so when the row broke out I beat it the other way. Made a noise as soon as I reckoned I was safe. Two of 'em chased me. It was a hunk of pie."

Peter demanded, "D'you know where they are now?"

"Two down below in the gully, one up on the hill beyond. Haven't seen the fourth."

"The one they call the Captain," said Peter, "the one with the quiet voice, he'll be down with the car. They're not using the headlamp by itself yet, but they must have un-shipped it by now."

"Reckon somebody'd see 'em from the road," Clinton offered. "Now what do we do?"

"I think we've still time to cross the Wall where we slept. They'll never find us down in the valley."

"I hope!" said Mig. "They've thirty thousand good reasons to try."

"What d'you mean?"

"The Captain—whoever he is—thinks it's worth thirty thousand pounds—we heard him."

The whistle this time was long and low. "How much is that in dollars?" Clinton made a rapid calculation and said at once, "Best part of a hundred grand. Better get goin'!"

"Must see where my two are first." Peter waited until the torch flashed again. "Right! We needn't hurry. Don't kick any stones!"

They moved cautiously down beside the Wall, testing each foothold. Within four minutes they were at the crossing place. Mig gave the dish to Clinton to hold and crept to the patch of scrub where they had hidden the rucksacks, whole ages ago it seemed. Hers had a light aluminum frame. She unbuckled the frame from it rapidly, opened it, pulled out a sweater, fumbled and found a torch, and then, opening the front pocket, whipped out a packet of chocolate and slipped it inside a shirt pocket.

She took the dish from Clinton, and he said, "You ran with *that*? Weighs a ton!"

"It felt like it." She pushed it inside the sweater and knotted the arms around it. Then she put it into the rucksack frame—she had planned this with Peter while they waited on the hilltop. When it was secure, she adjusted the straps and put it on. The great dish covered the whole of her back and more.

Peter fished for one or two things that he needed—a clasp knife, the cigarette lighter he carried instead of matches, a couple of handkerchiefs.

Clinton felt blindly and found a sweater. Before he had time to locate anything else, they heard voices.

Peter flicked at Mig. "Over! Quick!"

The Wall crossing was familiar now, home ground. They could feel their way without difficulty even in the darkness. She went across, climbing like a cat and as silently. Clinton followed her. Again there was no noise. It was Peter whose foot slipped, making a long scraping sound. It was followed at once by a bellow of rage, seemingly from above them. In a fraction of a second he was clear. They ran now without concealment, without bothering about noise, straight down the path, knowing how it headed, knowing that the darkness hid them.

The man on the hill began to shout to the other two—something about "blasted kids." He stopped, and they heard one of the others calling, his words indistinguishable—aimed, they guessed, at the leader down at the car. Behind them they heard somebody clattering over the Wall, and then a noise as he slipped and swore and recovered himself and began to blunder after them.

The slope was easing out below them, and they were running in flying strides. They agreed afterward that they had been enormously exhilarated at this point. They knew where the gaps were, they knew the lie of the country, they knew even the feel of the turf—and the man behind them didn't; he was only one man. Presently even the noise of his progress stopped, and after a little they slowed down and could hear voices shouting back and forth.

Peter reduced speed to a walk, a fast walk.

Clinton recovered his breath enough to ask, "What are we goin' to do?"

"Head for Bonnyrigg Hall," said Peter stoutly. "They'll help us."

Manson saw the car swing out of a gap at the side of the road as he came back from The Twice Brewed and turn toward him, its engine snarling in much too sudden acceleration. It had only one head lamp, and the beam glared at him like a searchlight.

He said mildly, as it passed him, "Ferruginous fool!" and drove on. He was moving slowly, half hoping to see the children sitting at the roadside or trudging (footsore, he trusted) along the side of it. But he was also looking for the gateway of the track that led to Housesteads Farm. He proposed to use it to get as far in to the valley as possible so that he could go to the dig first to ask the man on guard duty if he knew anything of the three and after that to go to Housesteads Farm. If something had gone wrong—if there had been a sprained ankle or a broken arm—they would have gone for help there. He refused to consider any kind of accident that could involve all three. It wasn't, he explained to himself, "on"—it just wasn't "on" at all.

He picked out the gate a little before he expected it, stopped the car off the road, climbed out, opened it, drove through it, stopped again, and closed it carefully behind him. He remembered that there was a miniature pass through the ridge alongside the road, and he thought he remembered a pond somewhere and that down at the bottom the road ran over level turf. In a minute or two he reached the turf, slowed almost to a stop, found a place where he could drive on to it, and turned back behind the end of the ridge. When he decided that he had gone far enough, he climbed out into absolute silence. For the moment traffic on the road had ceased; there was no wind; there were no bird noises even. The place was utterly peaceful, and far over to the east the moon was rising in a splendid golden glow.

He said half aloud, "I'm an ass to worry," and strode up toward the digging.

When he was about fifty yards away, he called out, "I want to speak to Professor Carrick's night guard!" He wished he knew who it was; the man's name would have been a safer introduction. There was no reply anyway. He said to himself, "Asleep," and shouted again, his voice louder. There was still no reply. Grumblingly to himself, he said, "Don't want a charge of bird shot in me," and bellowed loudly.

Suddenly he felt a cold trickle of fear go down the back of his neck. He moved forward more rapidly, shouting all the time for the night guard. The ruins themselves looked wholly peaceful, and he made for the hut, its blackness just beginning to be touched by the silver of the moon.

Blake was outside it, sprawled on the ground, quite unconscious.

The moon was beginning to reach down to them in the valley now. Peter said bitterly, "It *would* be full!"

"What of it?" Clinton shook his head. "Colors we're wearin' won't show up. Shall I take it now, Mig?"

"I was wondering when somebody was going to ask," said Mig frankly. She slipped off the pack and stood rubbing her shoulders where the straps had chafed. "There's a car up the valley."

"Going to Bonnyrigg, I expect."

Clinton adjusted the weight. They listened for a moment to the silence behind them. Whatever the enemy was doing, he was doing it quietly. They began to walk, their legs a little uncertain after the rest. "Where's it now?"

The car was hidden in a fold of the valley floor, but they could hear it faintly, enough for Peter to say, "Bonnyrigg road all right."

They walked on more cheerfully. If there was a car, there would be people. People meant help.

Peewits called over near the lake, and twice they heard wings overhead. Once something scuttled through the grass a few yards ahead of them, blundering in front until it suddenly acquired sense enough to turn off to the right.

Mig felt lighter, and lighter-hearted, without the weight of the dish. Her shoulders ached, but she felt as if she could go on walking all night. She wondered how Mr. Blake was. He'd told them to go on, but she wasn't sure. "Ought one of us to have stayed with Mr. Blake?" she asked suddenly.

"Who? Oh, Mr. Blake! He told us to go on." Peter's voice was worried.

"Wouldn't have done any good," said Clinton flatly. "The thugs went back past the dig; they'd have got whoever it was for sure."

"They'll say we should have stayed with him." Peter expressed the normal doubt of the young.

"If we've saved the dish?" Clinton laughed softly and then, without changing the level of his voice, added, "I suppose you know that automobile's only got one head-light?"

They stopped. There was a brief silence. Then Mig said in a small voice, enunciating the words with great care, "I think I'm going to be afraid."

"Won't do us any harm if we are," said Clinton philosophically. "Make us a bit more careful."

Peter stared at Mig. His forehead was wrinkled with worry. He was beginning to realize what they had let themselves in for—and it was his responsibility.

There was another small silence. Then Clinton asked, in an ordinary tone again, "How'd he get here so fast?"

"Came over the Peel Gap," replied Peter. "There's a side road to the north, goes back to Shield on the Wall. Then he must have turned on to the farm track to Bonnyrigg."

"How'd he know?"

"How'd he know there was a road, d'you mean?"

"Uh-huh."

"One of them could be a local man."

"In those clothes?" demanded Mig scornfully.

"How then?"

"Map." Mig's tone was final.

"Okay. Now how much do you remember of the map? How far does the farm track go?"

Peter answered him. "We crossed it just before we reached the lough this afternoon."

"It was kinda rough, wasn't it?"

Peter agreed.

"Sort of petering out?"

"I can't remember. I think it's a dead end just a bit beyond."

"Let's think this thing out." Clinton was silent for a long minute before he said, "If I was the top guy, I'd guess that we were heading for Bonnyrigg Hall. It's the one place he'd be sure we'd get help. Right? So I'd cover it, and let the others ride herd on us up toward it. Right? Then I'd make 'em close in somewhere far enough from the house to make sure we wouldn't be helped in time, and rush us, grab the dish, and bolt in the car. Right?"

"I suppose so," Peter agreed reluctantly. "But he can't do much by himself . . ."

"He's got the transport." Clinton spoke more to himself than to the others. "*And* he's got the light. I reckon he'll find him a piece of high ground, get out the light, and sweep and sweep until he picks us up."

Mig, half listening, and with the rest of her mind following and puzzling over the car as it moved unevenly along the road, said abruptly, "It's stopped."

Clinton stared at the malevolent beam of light that stretched out into the darkness. His voice was almost aggrieved as he demanded, "What in heck's he doin' that for?"

As he spoke, the car started again, moving fast to the east.

"Wasn't by himself," said Peter. "He's dropped somebody to watch Bonnyrigg and West Hotbank Farm. He's about midway between, and he's going on himself."

"How could he have someone else with him?" Mig's voice was unsure.

"One of them ran down the hill to him before he shot off," said Peter, working it out. "That's what all the shouting was about perhaps."

"What do we do now?" Mig's back felt cold, though she knew she was hot from the hard walking—cold and shivery.

"No use going on," said Peter, "not to Bonnyrigg. We've got to think of something else."

"Two chances," said Clinton promptly. "East? West?"

"What d'you mean?"

"They're in front of us; they're behind us." Clinton worked it out eagerly. "But they ain't on our sides yet. What happens if we go east?"

"Broomlee Lough," replied Peter. "Why?"

"Any houses? Anywhere there'd be people?"

"Housesteads."

"Sure." Clinton knocked his fist against the palm of his hand. "He'll reckon we'll head for there soon as we know we can't get to Bonnyrigg. So?"

"So we don't," said Peter. "We go west."

"Guy up there"—Clinton nodded to where the car had paused—"he'll be working down toward us by now."

Mig asked, "Where's the other Hotbank Farm?"

"Southwest . . ." began Peter.

"Southwest then," said Clinton sharply. "My pop says pick the unlikely one. You know where southwest is?"

"Polestar." Peter jerked his finger to the sky.

"Let's get this show on the road then."

They began to trot as silently as they could through the dry grass, heading down a slow, easy slope.

"Somebody's fetched you an almighty crack on the head," said Manson to the unconscious man, "but your pulse is all right, and you're breathing pretty well. I'm going to cover you up and get the police and an ambulance." He eased a folded blanket gingerly under Blake's head and covered him with a second. "It's a warm night, and the grass is dry. You won't come to any particular harm."

He straightened himself and strode over to the excavation. He could see at once that the dish was gone. He had been certain that it would be; but, even so, there was a sense of shock. He swore quietly to relieve his feelings, then turning, began to run diagonally across the slope to the car.

Six minutes later he was hammering at the Housesteads door.

Into the phone he said, "Hexham police! This is an emergency."

The wait seemed interminable—it was probably not more

than a matter of seconds—then he was talking to the station sergeant. He said urgently, "This is John Manson, the editor of *The Clarion*. I'm speaking from Housesteads Farm. I want police, an ambulance, and a doctor as fast as possible. . . ."

The voice interrupted him. "Manson . . . M—A—N—S—O—N?"

"Yes, yes!" snapped Manson impatiently. "A man has been attacked and seriously injured . . ."

"And the address is Housesteads Farm?" said the voice, implacable.

"For God's sake, yes! There are three children missing, and there has been a theft of . . ."

"Can you give me the name o' the man?"

"No! No, I can't," said Manson furiously. "But if you don't get an ambulance and a doctor moving within the next two minutes, I'll carry the story right across the front page of *The Clarion* tomorrow morning. Shut up and listen! Send the ambulance and the doctor to the old quarry gate, a mile beyond the Housesteads main entrance. There'll be somebody waiting to guide them there. As soon as you've done that get on to Inspector Weatherly, tell him John Manson says to get up here as fast as he can and with as many men as he can. Tell him *exactly* that—and don't alter one word of it!"

"Sir," said the voice, suddenly galvanized.

He put the phone down and said, "Can you get somebody to the old quarry gate to wait for them? And will you ring Professor Carrick and tell him what's happened?"

"The car's turning," Mig whispered. They'd given up speaking above a whisper.

Peter stopped and said urgently, "Down!"

They were in a patch of stunted bracken, but there was

enough to cover them. The single beam swung slowly round, sweeping clear across the slope on which they lay. Whoever was driving the car had picked his position with great skill. The beam seemed to flood the shallow valley. It swept over them, passed down into the hollow, and stopped. A long tongue of light filled the shallow valley bottom.

"Run!" Peter ordered. "And look out for the other light! He'll have that on us in a minute."

They began a hasty shambling plunge along the slope.

Afterward all three of them admitted to a feeling of panic at this point. "I was scairt," said Clinton candidly. "Just plumb scairt."

None the less it was he who slowed them down. Looking back over his shoulder, he saw the second light begin to sweep over the moorland. The Captain—they were positive now he was driving the car—was covering the ground on the Housesteads side. Clinton said, "Easy! Go easy now! He's working the other end. We guessed right. Wouldn't do us a helluva lot o' good to break a leg."

They eased down to a fast walk. They were all breathless, all uncertain, all desperately glad of the relief. They walked in Indian file, Peter leading, Clinton with the dish in the middle, Mig close behind him.

It was Mig who said, suddenly optimistic, "Dad'll have the police there by now."

The boys accepted it. No one wanted to question a possibility of hope.

13

The patrol car arrived first. Manson saw the light sweep round as it came in to the gate. It stopped for what seemed an inordinate length of time and then turned down the track toward the bottom of the slope. He bent over Blake, who was breathing uneasily and heavily. "Won't be long now, old chap." He had found Blake's torch, and he walked over to the edge of the excavation, blinking it in the direction of the police car to indicate the position. He watched the car turn and head toward the vallum, its headlights lurching over the landscape.

It went on past the point where the vallum disappeared, paused for the gate in the dry-stone wall, and turned up toward him, its gears complaining. Just short of the excavation it stopped.

He went over to it hurriedly. "I'm John Manson. Is the ambulance coming?"

The policeman who opened the door said, "It'll be coming, sir. We were told to report here and that a man had been attacked."

"He's here." Manson flashed the torch back towards Blake. "He's been coshed, I think. They've stolen a big silver dish . . ."

"Message didn't say anything about a burglary," said the policeman, and over his shoulder: "Not a word about that, Charlie?"

"Not a word," agreed Charlie.

"Where did they steal it from?"

"The excavation," Manson answered, moving with the two men toward Blake.

"Wouldn't be burglary then," said the driver, "not house-breaking neither. Just theft or summut."

"Well, the summut will be something in the region of a good few thousand pounds," retorted Manson grimly.

"Would it now?" said the driver with a new tone of respect coming into his voice. "This how you found him?"

"No," replied Manson shortly. "He was lying on his face. I turned him over and got the blanket under him. He's not too good."

"Better get back and call the information room!" The driver turned to Manson. "There was something about three children."

"There was." Quite suddenly and with a tremor of fear Manson realized that he had almost forgotten the children. The urgency of Blake's condition, the disappearance of the dish, the infuriating slowness of the station sergeant, had put them out of his mind but at the back of it. He went on, "Three of them—two of them mine, the third an American boy of fourteen. They should have phoned from The Twice Brewed at eight o'clock."

"It's a quarter to ten now. Would they ha' been here?"

"Not after dark," said Manson, anxiety suddenly flooding over him.

The driver left him without comment. Manson heard him saying, "Three children. Should have phoned from The Twice Brewed—eight o'clock. Tell 'em to make inquiries."

And then, straightening up and looking along the road to Newcastle, "That'll be the ambulance."

Manson turned and said soberly, "Thank God for that!"

Peter muttered sharply, "Down!" and dropped on to the bare turf. Before the others could question him, he whispered, "Somebody flashing a light up the slope."

They followed the line of his hand. A torch was flashing on and off, perhaps two hundred yards to the right of them and a little ahead.

"Must have been close behind us all the time," said Peter bitterly. They peered ahead over the difficult moonlit country. "There's a ridge of some sort. If we could get to that, he'd lose us for a bit."

"Aren't there some trees somewhere?" asked Mig.

"May be able to see them from the ridge," Peter answered hopefully. "If we can get through before the character who was dropped from the car gets down, we'll have 'em all behind us."

"We can try," grunted Clinton.

"Can you run?" Peter turned to Mig.

"I can run," she replied stoutly.

"Right! Let's go!"

They hurtled down the last of the hill, passed over the hollow between the main slope and the ridge, and running like frightened hares, got to the north face of it.

Halfway along it Clinton said, "Stop sharp when I say and listen. Now!"

Above the beating of their hearts and the wheeze of their breathing they heard, well away up to the right and a little behind them, the sound of heavy boots crashing across the dry grass.

"The car guy. T'other one must be behind us. We're through if we can keep runnin'."

Peter said, "Give me that thing now! You've had your go."

"Sure," agreed Clinton, "sure!"

They changed over, and Peter led off at once, picking the best ground that he could see. After a little he whispered back over his shoulder, "Trees." He couldn't remember them at all from the map. He was no longer confident, in fact, of their position in relation to the map. They were a long way from Hotbank Farm and safety—that much he knew, and that was enough. He altered course for the trees; they might at least give a chance of rest in shelter. They were perhaps three hundred yards away. Peter, as he ran, wondered if they could last three hundred yards. The sweat was streaming into his eyes now. He remembered long cross-country runs at school, but they'd never done anything like the distances that the three of them had done today. He wasn't sure that his legs really belonged to him any longer. He began to worry about Mig.

Then quite suddenly the trees were enormous, and they were almost under their shadow, and he realized that there was only a thin line of them, hardly more than a windbreak. They stood up like a column of soldiers, and he gasped out, "Which side do we go?"

"No time to toss." Clinton's voice was wheezing. "The car'll be coming back. Better make it the south side—the lights."

They staggered on perhaps fifty yards and collapsed, wholly exhausted, in the bracken and bramble of the tree edge.

When she could speak, Mig said, "But where would he tell them to look?"

"Who?" Peter almost groaned.

"The police." Mig swallowed in an effort to make her voice clearer.

Wearily Peter remembered her earlier optimism. "Dunno," he said despairingly.

"But what exactly," asked the Inspector, "were *you* doing here?"

"Looking for my young," replied Manson, with a faint trace of irritation. "I told you." He had gone through the whole thing painstakingly, movement by movement, to the finding of the unconscious Blake.

Inspector Weatherly said: "But why here?"

"This was their finishing point," explained Manson carefully. "I knew that Carrick would have a night guard on the place. He was the nearest person who would have any knowledge of them, if they *had* reached here. I came up to ask him."

"And you knew about this dish?"

"Carrick showed it to me."

"You didn't pass the news on?"

"I did not." Manson tried to keep the irritation out of his voice. "Carrick told me about it privately."

"Did they know about it?"

"I don't know. I don't know if they got here. That was what I was trying to find out."

"But if they did get here, Carrick would have told them about it?"

"He'd have shown them," said Manson wearily, unable to see what the Inspector was driving at. "He's a friend of theirs."

"They must be pretty tough?" There was an upward inflection at the end of Weatherly's words that made the sentence a question rather than a supposition.

"They are," replied Manson shortly.

Weatherly's voice was mild as he said, "Must have been best part of fifteen-twenty miles over the moors the way they came. Do you often let 'em go on escapades like this?"

"It wasn't an escapade." Manson felt that he was being pushed on to the defensive. "It was a perfectly sound attempt at an historical reconstruction. Carrick argued that the Wall was proof against small infiltrations, and Peter said that he would get across it. That was all—they were trying to prove a case."

"Would they know the value of a thing like that?"

"Of course they'd know the value of it!" Manson snorted indignantly.

"Is your boy going to be a newspaperman?" Weatherly changed the line of his questions abruptly.

"No," snapped Manson. "Why?"

"Make a sensational story," mused Weatherly. "School-children find greatest Roman treasure."

"You mean you think *they* took it? You miserable flatfoot! You—you . . . pavement pounder! Heaven help me, I thought you were a friend of mine! You're a uniform, that's all—a uniform!"

"They were headed for here." Weatherly disregarded Manson's outburst. "If they got here, they were shown the thing. Nobody else knew about it except yourself. Now it's gone."

"And I suppose they coshed him?" Manson demanded bitterly.

"We don't know that he *was* coshed," said the Inspector mildly. "He may have been running after somebody in the dark and fallen and hit his head against one of these blocks of stone. We'll examine 'em in the morning."

"He was yards away from the blocks."

"The doctor said he'd crawled a distance."

"Supposing he did? How does that bring in my children?"

Weatherly gave him the point. "It doesn't. But somebody knew about the dish. They couldn't have found it in the dark without knowledge. And, on your showing, only Carrick's people and yourself and possibly your children knew."

"They couldn't have done it," said Manson simply and with absolute sincerity. "How *can* you say that?"

Weatherly attacked again rapidly. "You know what kids are nowadays. You know the sort of things they get up to. They wouldn't have thought that there was any harm in it. They might have been trying to steal a march on Carrick."

Manson all of a sudden was immensely tired. He said wearily, "You wouldn't understand, you policeman, but Peter has a feeling for history—he lives it sometimes—it's deep in him. He wouldn't have pulled that thing out of the excavation any more than he'd grab the cross off the high altar of Durham. But you wouldn't be able to see that."

"We've got to consider it," insisted Weatherly doggedly. "What about the American boy?"

"I don't know," Manson admitted, for the first time faintly uncertain. "He's quiet, intelligent . . ." The idea suddenly made him angry. "No, he wouldn't do it any more than the other two. He's a good kid."

"How d'you tell 'em nowadays?" asked Weatherly. "He might have put 'em up to it. Give him something to talk about when the holidays were over—how they beat the professionals to it."

"You're wrong!" Manson burst out passionately. "You're utterly, absolutely, horribly wrong! Where are they now?"

"If I were a kid and I'd done it, I would've nipped smartly down the road to Bardon Mill and caught the bus for Newcastle."

"And what would three children do at midnight in Newcastle? I doubt if they had more'n a pound between 'em."

"Not Newcastle then." Weatherly thought for a minute.

"This was a raid. Supposing they'd decided to make it realistic. Suppose they took it to Carrick at Hexham to prove their case?"

"No," said Manson desperately. "You don't understand. You can't understand! It would be archaeological sacrilege."

"I don't think I'd have known what the words 'archaeological sacrilege' meant at fifteen."

"No"—Manson looked at him long in the moonlight—"you wouldn't."

Slowly their breathing settled down, the heart pounding stopped. They were normal, healthy young. The knowledge of escape—even if it was only temporary—had its effect. They were no longer desperately afraid.

Mig heard the car first. The gang must have had some agreed system of signaling.

"How does the road go?" demanded Clinton.

"Not so far from the end of the trees, I should think," Peter answered slowly.

"If I were the head guy," said Clinton, "I'd bring the car as close to the west end of the trees as I could, and I'd fix the light so that we couldn't break across it, and I'd beat up the line of the trees with the three of them. What with the car lights and the moon we shouldn't have a dog's chance."

Mig said abruptly, "So?" She was beginning to know how Clinton's mind worked.

"So we get out now, and we nip along the north edge. It looks steeper that side, and we get as low down as possible. He can't use the spotlight while he's drivin'. We get as close to the road as we can as soon as the car's passed us— just as soon—we beat it across the road like bats out of hell."

"What about the man he dropped on the way up?" asked Peter.

"He'll want to yak with the guy who's flashin' the torch. He's a city guy. They always want to yak when they're in the country. Scared of the wide open . . . Let's move!" He groaned painfully. "Lordy, how's ma po' laigs!"

Mig almost managed a giggle.

They found a way through the belt of trees. Beyond it they discovered an expanse of young firs. They were perhaps three feet high and spaced widely enough so that they offered no obstacle but promised instead cover in an emergency. The three were across them in two minutes; at the edge of the grown trees beyond, they stopped and peered out cautiously.

The car was well down from Bonnyrigg Hall now. It was moving slowly.

Clinton said, "We can do it—have a minute in hand even."

He slipped quietly out of the trees. The moon shadow hid them a long way down the slope. Then they ran silently in the open. They could see the glow of the single headlight but not the light itself. So far they were safe. The shallow depression took them almost up to the farm track. Just short of it Clinton flung himself down in a patch of bracken, and the others followed suit. A moment later the fern was brilliant in the beam of the light. A straight sector of the road held it on them for what seemed an intolerable time, and then, as the car followed a curve, it swept away, and the car purred slowly past them. It was scarcely clear when Clinton heaved himself up and ran, bent double, across the moonlit road. One by one the others followed him. They ran on for a hundred yards, found a depression once again filled with stunted bracken, and dropped in it. Clinton stayed on one knee, watching. Presently the car stopped. The engine switched off. One headlight beamed south down the slope, the other at right angles to it along the north face of the trees. It was a neat enough trap. Clinton surveyed it with satisfaction.

At last he said, "Sneak up thataway!" He pointed to the west. "I'll catch up with you."

"Where are you going?" demanded Peter.

"I collect distributor heads," Clinton answered dreamily. "If I can see where the Cap'n's got to, I'm goin' to add to my collection. Keep movin' but not too fast, and make with the bird noises, Mig."

For the first time for hours Mig laughed.

14

The Professor strode into the circle of light like an angry general. He ignored the Inspector, brushed past him, and stopping in front of Manson, said, his voice barking and quite unlike its usual gentle tone, "Have they found your three yet?"

"They have *not!*" Manson matched his anger with his own. "The Inspector thinks that they stole the silver dish and knocked out your night guard."

The Professor rounded on the Inspector. "I never heard such infernal clotted nonsense in my life! His two are friends of mine. They would no more do a thing like that than—than burn a church."

The Inspector said inconsequently, "You use the same sort of comparison." And then, more officially but his voice quite reasonable, "All the same, they're missing; the dish is missing; and your man's unconscious."

"Blake? He'll be all right. The doctor told the lad at the gate to tell me. What have you done about the youngsters?"

The Inspector abruptly became official. "I've started inquiries," he answered, blocking further questions. "They *were* here?"

"Of course they were here!" said Carrick brusquely. "Spent the best part of the day here." He looked over toward Manson. "I owe you a fiver, and they know it."

"So they saw the dish. They knew where it was?"

"Of course they did!"

"And they knew how to shift the blocks that were holding it pinned?"

"They're intelligent," said Carrick.

"Then they could have moved them with a crowbar and got away with the dish?"

"They could *not*, you purblind policeman!" The Professor had reached precisely the level of indignation that Manson had attained in the first part of his interview. "Listen! That child greased her hand, eased it in behind the dish, and spent half an hour telling us in detail about the figures on the face of it. I've never listened to anything so beautifully done. It was poetry and—and, dammit, it was love! That child would no more harm a thing as precious as that than—than—oh, heavens, I can't think of a comparison! You don't understand. She feels about these things."

The Inspector said, "There are two boys. They could have overridden her."

"Mig? Overriden Mig? You don't know that young woman! That's the whole trouble. You don't *know*—you can't know. The American boy's a good level-headed youngster. I don't know him, but I know the others. They would no more risk anything that would harm a masterpiece like that dish . . . Ah, what's the use? Has it occurred to you, Inspector, that they may have surprised the thieves and be trying to follow them—and getting damn little support from you and your people?"

The Inspector jerked his head round swiftly. "It has not!" He waited for a brief moment and said almost humbly, "It ought to have, but it has not. Tell me, what time did they reach you this morning?"

"About a quarter past nine, I would think."

"And they came?"

"Over the gap at Cuddys' Crag, down, covered by the shoulder there"—he indicated the slope of the hill behind his back—"and then stalked us, using the hut. Mig was standing alongside me a full minute before I saw her."

"And then?"

"They stayed with us all through the day helping, and remarkably helpful they were too, and we got Mig to tell us everything that she could find out about the face of the dish, and the boys carted spoil."

"They ate with you?"

"At lunchtime, yes."

"And in the afternoon?"

"They worked with us until we knocked off."

"*Then* where did they go?"

"They said they were hot and wanted to have a swim before they phoned from The Twice Brewed."

Manson, holding himself tensely silent during the dialogue, broke out harshly, "A swim!" All through the evening he had comforted himself with the certainty that no accident could have involved all three of them simultaneously. No accident—except a swimming accident. Almost deliberately he had excluded drowning from his mind. "Where were they going to swim?"

Carrick said, "Peter's pretty good, isn't he? And Mig?"

"She swims well, fairly well."

"And the American boy?"

"I asked him before he crossed the river. He said he'd been able to swim since he was six—something like that."

The Inspector asked, "Where were they going?"

"Over the gap and down to Greenlee Loff. I told them to head for the Jenkins Burn and to turn right where it enters the loff—there's a rough track there, leads to a little beach."

The Inspector said, "Sergeant Belsay!" The sergeant came

over. More loudly the Inspector called, "Is there anybody here who could guide the sergeant to the Jenkins Burn?"

One of the men from Housesteads said, "I know it."

"Take a walkie-talkie. Get over to this beach fast! Let us know anything you can. You won't be able to do much before dawn; do what's possible."

"I'll go with him," said Manson.

"You'll be more use to us here." The rasp had gone out of the Inspector's voice. "The patrols are working along the roads now—Carlisle has set up a roadblock at Warwick Bridge."

"My God!" exclaimed Manson. "I never told you. It went absolutely out of my mind."

"What?"

"A car—a car with one headlight. Just before I got to the corner for Bardon Mill. It came into the road from the north side—must have been from the old quarry path. I thought it was somebody who'd been parked at the road-side. It went past me in a hurry."

"And turned down for Bardon Mill?"

"No." Manson was digging desperately into his mind for the memory. "No, it went straight on. I remember checking its rear lights in the mirror."

Weatherly said somberly, "Pity we didn't have this earlier." He called down to the patrol car, "Ask the information room to put out a general call—all cars, ours and Carlisle's—they'll be listening in on our wavelength: 'Pick up any car with one head lamp.'"

Clinton wormed his way along the ditch at the side of the road for another six feet. When he raised his head again, he was opposite the driver's door. Very cautiously he worked himself into a position from which he could see the Captain between the wheels. He was about thirty feet away, standing on a rock strategically placed exactly between the beams of light. He stood absolutely still, watching. The whole plan showed a clear-thinking professional mind—a ruthless mind. Clinton shivered.

He had two alternatives. Almost certainly the keys would have been left in the car. He could snatch them and run, and the men would need twenty minutes or so before they would be able to short-circuit the ignition wiring—but they could, he was certain, do it in the end. He could have done it himself if he had had to. The other alternative was to get the distributor head. To do that he needed to get the hood open without being heard. The night was very still. All hoods, he knew, made a sharp click, a metallic noise, on opening and he had first to find the release catch. This was a British car—wholly unfamiliar. He thought for a moment and knew that he would have to try for both. The keys first—then, if the man on the rock heard the hood opening, he would still have time to run, and the car would be out of action for twenty minutes at least. If he were able to do both, it would be out till daylight.

He raised himself inch by inch to the level of the windows. As his hand came above the rim, he saw the Captain move suddenly and froze. The man was sharply clear in the glare of the lights—medium height, athletic-looking, in hard condition. He had a military air; he carried himself like an officer—perhaps he was an officer—an ex-officer, heading a gang. It happened. He changed position again, disregarding whatever it was that had caught his attention. The stillness of his head indicated that his eyes were fixed on the edge of the trees like those of a watchful leopard.

Again Clinton shivered. He dared not look down at the dashboard. With both his own eyes firmly on the back of the Captain's head, he slipped in his arm, felt delicately along until a fingertip touched something loose, and there was the faintest clink of metal. He had eased the key half out when he saw a figure move in the edge of the beam of light that shone at right angles to the road. Clearly this was what the Captain had seen earlier.

The steely voice said, "You're slipping, Cleave. If I'd been an enemy, you'd have had a bullet through you twice. You've lost them."

"They got away, Cap'n."

Under cover of the voices Clinton pried out the keys, moved crouching to the end of the car, and fumbled under the radiator grille for the hood release.

He heard the leader's voice again. "Comb out the last clump!"

As he reached the word "clump," Clinton's fingers found the release and pulled it. The catch came free, the noise much louder than he had expected, but there was no move from the Captain. Carefully he eased up the hood, felt inside, and more by luck than by judgment found what he believed to be the distributor head. It clicked as he released it, and again he froze. There was still no movement on the rock. He could hear the man Cleave crashing through the undergrowth beyond. He put his finger inside and felt round, pulling at anything loose. Something cut his finger, and he breathed, "Blast!" All the time his eyes were on the still head lit in the glow of the lights. There was no movement even when he stole away, his eyes fixed on the moonlit ground to avoid noise.

He had made good barely a hundred yards when he heard a voice bellow, "Cap'n, the car!"

He put his head down and began to run—fast. They would be making enough noise themselves as they rushed to the car to drown the sound of his feet in the grass. He had, he reckoned, perhaps a minute before they would be able to get the headlight trained so that it would cover the area through which he ran.

He was given barely three quarters of a minute. Then, out of the corner of his eye, he was aware of the beam of light well to the right sweeping over towards the trees in which Bonnyrigg stood. Slowing down so that he would not fall, he ran with his head over his shoulder, judging the movement of the beam. When he guessed that it was sweeping back to him, he dived for cover.

The Captain held the head lamp. Methodically, he was working down the slope from Bonnyrigg, swinging in a slow arc from north to northwest to west.

Behind him the man Cleave was gibbering with rage. "Damn kids!" he muttered over and over again. "They nicked the keys and they've done something under the bonnet. Can't see . . ."

The third man joined them, breathing hard, clearly out of condition. "What's up?"

"Blasted kids," explained Cleave.

Beyond the car the Captain said, "Quiet! D'you want half the farms in the valley down on us? There's been too much noise as it is."

"Sir," said the third man, responding automatically to the tone.

The fourth man came running down the road to them in the glare of the other head lamp.

The Captain, still sweeping slowly round with the light, spoke without turning. "Edwards, find out what they've done to the car! See if you can start it!"

The man Cleave called, "Something there. Hold it!"

A bird rocketed up through the beam of light almost incandescent for a moment in its brilliance and disappeared into the safe darkness overhead.

The Captain swept back with the light over the segment of the circle that he had already covered.

From the hood of the car Edwards' voice came muffled. "Distributor 'ead's gone."

"Can you do anything about it?"

"Take time," said Edwards.

"Right!" The Captain's voice was still cold and steady. "We'll try it another way then. Switch off the lights!" Somebody fumbled at the dashboard, found the switch, and turned it. The moonlight seemed for an instant very dark. "Edwards, get down the road, find a place where we can run her into the trees. Wait there and signal me in. Cleave, you and Dent move up the road—at the double. If you hear anybody coming from the farms, keep clear. They've gone that way"—he gestured to the northwest— "I'm quite certain. Keep between them and the forest. Move quietly—you'll hear them make a noise sooner or later. Don't let them hear you! You used to be able to do it on patrol." There was a cutting edge to his voice now. Turning, he climbed into the driving seat. "Get me moving before you go!"

The car gathered momentum on the slight slope. For perhaps fifty yards it ran faster and faster. Then he was aware of Edwards in the moonlight signaling with his right hand. He turned just short of him; the car ran jerkily over a slight turf bank and then pitched down a steep incline. He saw trees ahead of him and dark shadow, selected a gap with instant decision, and plunged into it. The car came to a grating halt, three quarters covered by the trees. He slipped from the wheel, closed the door without banging it, and strode back to the man Edwards.

He said confidently, "They're heading northwest. Keep over a little to the west and get between them and any trees you see. Dent and Cleave will be to the eastward. I'll be in the middle. They're bound to make a noise some time. Listen for it!"

As they came to the top of the little rise, Mig turned her head back. "The lights are out."

"He's done it then!" said Peter exultantly.

"*And* got away!"

"How d'you know?" demanded Peter.

"Stands to reason. If they could work the car, they'd have the other headlight over this way. They'd know we were here because of him."

"He wouldn't tell."

"Of course he wouldn't tell, but they'd know. We'd have to be here. If they'd heard him getting away, they'd still be using the lights, but they're not." She made the nightjar call, so realistically and so suddenly that Peter jumped, startled. There was no reply.

"Come on!" said Peter. "We said we'd keep moving."

"D'you think they have . . . ?"

"No. I think you're right. He's fast."

15

"Blank," said the Inspector, "absolute blank. Nobody's seen three children. Nobody's seen a car with one headlight. The barmaid at The Twice Brewed thinks she heard a car go up the Peel road about the time you left, but it might have been before, and she didn't take any notice of it anyway. There was a good deal of traffic on the main road."

"Where does the Peel road go to?" asked Manson. "Kielder, isn't it?"

"No, dead end," said the Inspector flatly. "Goes back over Shield on the Wall. But we've been on to Kielder—they've seen nothing. Ordinary traffic, that's all."

The Professor came over to them. Sadly, in the light of a powerful torch, he had been contemplating the space where the dish had been. Earth, violently dislodged as the blocks of stone were wrenched away, had fallen in little avalanches in the beds where they had lain.

"It's a mess—it's a criminal mess!" He was silent for a moment and then added, "One more day, that was all we needed—one more day."

Manson said, "I'm terribly sorry about it, but you'll be able to check in the daylight."

"It doesn't seem much use." Carrick spoke wearily. "It's gone." His face was very drawn in the moonlight. Slowly, his voice hardly more than a whisper, he went on. "They couldn't sell it, you know. Nobody would buy a thing like that—nobody in the sort of world we live in."

"You know better than that, Professor." The Inspector's voice was faintly unsympathetic. "There was the Hillshield vase, and the casket at Angmering Castle last year—and the year before, there were at least five pieces that could never have been sold on the open market."

"The mad collector?" asked Manson doubtfully.

"More than one of 'em, and they're not mad," said the Inspector calmly. "They want things—want them badly enough to pay through the nose for them."

"But the value of a piece like this depends on its provenance, on its authenticity, on the moment of its finding."

"Does it?" asked the Inspector wryly. "Ask Interpol! There's money in ancient art as an investment, these days. Big money!"

"And if they couldn't sell it?"

"Melt it down for its silver value."

"Not a piece like *this!*"

"I don't think it'll comfort you, but if this is a professional job, they won't have to melt it. They'll have a purchaser lined up and waiting."

A voice called from the squad car. The Inspector got up and hurried over. They heard him talking for three long minutes; then he came back again. His voice very grave, he said, "Your Mr. Blake has been conscious for a few minutes."

"Is he all right?"

"He's conscious," repeated the Inspector. "He spoke."

"What did he say, man?" demanded Manson. "For heaven's sake, what did he say?"

"He said"—the Inspector spoke very slowly, very distinctly—" 'The children tried . . .' He didn't finish the sentence and neither the doctor nor my man could make out the next words. Then he said 'They stunned me.' And then he mentioned your daughter's name, Mr. Manson. But they couldn't distinguish any more—just the name Mig."

Manson buried his head in his hands. He said desperately, "It could mean anything. You can't take a few words—a few incomplete phrases . . ."

The Inspector interrupted grimly, "It *could* mean anything." This time he emphasized the word "could." "But they *were* here, you see. We don't need to bother about the lough now. They were here"—he paused for a moment, choosing his words very carefully—"and they didn't stay to help Blake. . . ."

Clinton said cheerfully, "You make as much noise as a herd of buffalo."

The other two stopped in their tracks, and Mig fell to her knees. "We thought we'd lost you. Oh, Clint, we thought we'd lost you! And I'm so tired. . . ."

Peter slipped the rucksack off his back and put the ponderous thing down with care. "D'you think it's safe to have a spell?"

Clinton grunted. "They're a crummy lot. They'd make a sight more noise than you, and I haven't heard a thing."

"Take foive," said Mig gratefully, imitating a television favorite.

They lay stretched out, quite silent, until at last Mig said, "You did it, Clint!"

"Taking candy from a kid. I hooked their ignition keys, and I pinched the distributor head. I don't think they'll find a way round that till the morning." Clinton took it out of his pocket and held it up in the moonlight for them to see. Then he skimmed it away from him up the slope and to the left. "Don't see why they should have it even if they catch us."

"Did you see any of them?"

"I watched the Captain for two minutes. He scares me."

"Is he big?"

"Medium. Army pattern. Holds himself like a gun. He doesn't shout. There was a second man—*he* was big. The Captain called him Cleave. G.I. type, not heavy on brain. Didn't see the others. I was runnin' like a cold in the head," he finished coarsely.

"What'll they do now?"

Clinton thought carefully for a long minute; then he said laconically, "Come after us." And, after another pause, "That one won't give up."

"What do we do then?"

"We could try to get back towards Bonnyrigg." Clinton considered this carefully. "If I was the Captain, first thing I'd do would be to send a coupla men up to see we didn't. That's where he put the light first. We might do it—we might walk into a trap."

Peter muttered slowly, almost to himself, "I think he'd want to keep us away from trees—from the plantations— after what happened down there."

"Could be," Clinton agreed with him. "If we knew how the trees lay . . ."

"We don't," said Peter grimly, "and the map's not much use in the moonlight. Best thing would be to head up toward the forest. Where we camped last night would be the place. If we could get into the Greenlee plantation . . ."

"Know where it is?"

Peter sagged. "No. We've twisted and turned."

Mig said, "There's forest north of us—must be—and we've still got the polestar."

"North then," said Clinton, rising.

Mig climbed wearily to her feet, stretched out, and caught hold of the rucksack straps. For a moment it seemed to her as if she could not lift the weight of it. Then common sense came back.

"I'll take it," Peter offered.

Mig grunted, "It's my turn; it's on already," and settled the straps to suit her shoulders. Her legs had been tired before, but now they were so stiff that she thought she would be unable to bend them. They ached all the way down. Her back ached with them.

Peter took the lead, finding the star at once.

It was Peter ten minutes later who heard the noise—the irregular crunch, crunch, crunch, of heavy feet over rough ground. It was over to the left of them and farther up the slope than the line that they had chosen. He held out his hands to stop the other two, and they stood drooping, desperately weary, listening to the sound.

It was while they stood that Mig saw the dark mass of the trees over to their right. Her mouth was dry but she moistened it enough to whisper, "Greenlee Forest—over there!"

Peter was in no way sure that it was Greenlee Forest, but it *was* forest and any trees now spelled hope. The boot noises were over to the left. This would take them clear if they were not sighted in the moonlight. He whispered back, "We can make it if we hurry. I know we can!"

Mig plodded on behind him, hardly able to think now, hardly able to feel. She walked automatically, pressed down by the load, bent down, swaying sometimes. Peter kept remorselessly ahead.

Slowly, almost imperceptibly, the dark pine trees grew darker, more solid; their crests began to show clear against the skyline. The moon shadow was immensely black.

Peter wiped the sweat out of his eyes and stared and

stared and stared, trying to find something that he could recognize, but there was nothing here save a wall of trees, a cliff, a barricade, a rampart. If they could get to them, they would be safe. If they could hide in them, they would be safe. He kept saying the words over and over to himself as they plodded on and on and on.

They were close to the woods when Clinton spotted the gate. He said, "The end of the path we came through."

It wasn't. It was altogether another gate, the entrance to another path, but he never knew it then or after.

It was Mig who saw the burn, and they dropped on their knees beside it and splashed water up to their mouths and over their faces and over their arms.

It was Peter who drove them on again toward the safety of the gate. Mig was behind. It had been difficult for her to get up from the waterside with the weight on her back. She felt pinned down by it, as if somebody were trying to hold her on the ground. She was five full paces behind as they entered the moon shadow. The shot hit her fairly in the middle of her back. The great silver dish rang for a moment like a gong, and she fell forward on her face.

16

Peter was with her almost as she fell. He said, his voice terrified, "Mig! Mig!"

Her breathing was wildly irregular, great wheezing gasps, choking sounds in her throat. Her hands were clawing at the ground.

He said again, "Mig! Mig! Did it hit you?"

Clinton had disappeared. Above the noise of the girl's desperate attempts to get breath, Peter heard his voice shouting a furious stream of abuse and threat.

Peter tried to turn Mig over, and the great dish got in the way. Hurriedly he slipped a strap down Mig's arm and pulled the framework away, letting it fall clear of her body. He remembered the clang of metal, and he began to feel her back. It was wet and hot. He thought, Blood; she's wounded. He said, "Mig, can you speak?" He put his hand inside her shirt. It was wetter still, stickier, but he could feel nothing —no wound, no broken flesh. "Please, Mig," he begged, "please—will you tell me where it is?"

Beyond Clinton a man shouted, and Peter half turned. He could just see Clinton straighten himself and fling something—a stone he guessed—and then another and another.

There was a quick yelp of pain and a grunt, and the man's voice came clearly, "You . . . ," and cut off before it reached the second word.

He heard Clinton, furious and triumphant, shouting, "Got him! Got him! ! Got him! ! !"

The American boy came running back.

Peter said despairingly, "It hit her. She's hurt. I think she's bleeding, but I can't find a wound."

The chaos of Mig's breathing had subsided a little. It was a deep broken wheezing now.

"Get her into the moonlight," suggested Clinton. "We can see then."

They put their hands under her arms and lifted her, and half carrying, half dragging her, hurried into the light. Peter pulled up her shirt. Her back was glistening but not with blood. He looked, puzzled, at his own hand. "Sweat! She isn't bleeding."

Clinton said, "It hit the dish. I heard it. Knocked the breath out of her."

Mig got her wind back with a last desperate heave. "Couldn't breathe," she gasped, "couldn't breathe."

"D'you think you can move?"

She took two more shuddering breaths. " 'Course!"

"We'd better beat it," said Clinton. "He'll come round in a minute. I rocked him, the s.o.b.—I rocked him good!"

Peter raced across the stream, picked up the dish and put on the framework fumbling as he ran back. "I ought to have been carrying it," he said remorsefully.

"Then she'd have had it for sure!" barked Clinton. "Up, Mig!"

The two boys got her under the arms again, hauled her to her feet, and began to run with her clumsily. Well down the slope they could hear the Captain's voice, sharp now and urgent, and from far away to the left the voice of the man with the heavy feet answering him. Where was the fourth? The hunt was closing in.

"If there was someone in the fire tower . . ." began Peter.

"At night?"

"No, I don't suppose till dawn."

"Getting near dawn," panted Clinton, squinting over his right shoulder. There was a grayness beginning in the east that did not belong to the moon.

"Not near enough." Peter sounded despairing.

Clinton asked, "You all right, Mig?"

"Yes." Her voice was still wheezing.

"Good girl! Good girl!" said Clinton approvingly. "How about our heading over for the tower anyway?"

Peter grunted, and they swung the girl round to the right. They were at the tongue of the wood now. Perhaps there was still a chance. They could see the main forest beyond them. It was vague and uncertain in the moonlight, with no deep shadow to make it stand out—but it was the forest, and the forest was safety.

They ran in a curious dragging lockstep, like a three-legged race. Every movement was an effort now. Their legs were aching, their backs stiff, even their arms were stiff and sore. They had long since stopped thinking about the beating of their hearts. Only the dryness of their mouths had disappeared with the hasty drink at the Greenlee Burn.

It was Mig who saw the fourth man. He was no more than a gray shadow moving against the more solid substance of the forest edge. "There! There! D'you see him?"

The boys saw him and altered course again without even bothering to ask each other, moving with one mind.

Mig said, "Let me go! I can run by myself now. It knocked the breath out of me—nothing else."

"The dish saved you," said Peter with enormous seriousness.

They ran on, the three of them considering this point, not speaking, but thinking the same way—wondering what would have happened but for the thick honest silver of the Roman platter.

It was Peter who first felt the squelch of water under his feet.

The sergeant dropped the rucksack on the turf. "Other two have boys' gear in 'em. This one was the girl's—no shoulder straps." He bent down and flicked over the open leather loops. "Fitted to one of those frames," he explained. "Somebody took it off in a hurry."

Manson said, "That's right. It was a light aluminum frame. We were trying it out. She liked it."

Weatherly asked soberly, "Where exactly was it, sergeant?"

"In the dip—just short of the Wall, this side. Didn't see 'em when we went over in the dark. Caught a glimpse of one of the boy's bags as we came back."

"Why would she take the frame and leave the bag?" The Inspector, on his haunches beside it, looked up at Manson.

Carrick said quickly, "Bathing things."

Manson shook his head. "They didn't have any."

The Inspector only grunted. "Did you see anything over there—anything at all—that was out of the ordinary?"

"No, sir," replied the sergeant stolidly. "One car on the Peel road, sir—only saw that for a moment. Nothing else."

The youth from Housesteads said, "I thought I heard something, Inspector."

"What?"

"Sounded like a shot."

"The sergeant didn't hear it?"

"No," said the sergeant, "I didn't hear it."

Everybody was silent for a long moment.

The youth said, "Deer poachers, it could have been. You get them on moonlight nights."

"A shot?" Manson's face was haggard. The naked fear showed for a moment in his eyes.

Carrick said, "There's a deal of poaching in this area—day *and* night."

The Inspector murmured, "Could be."

They all stared fascinated at the strapless rucksack.

"I'd say"—the Inspector's voice was quiet and dispassionate—"that she got something out of it hurriedly, took it off the frame, and didn't bother to close it properly. What did she want with the frame?"

"For heaven's sake!" exclaimed Carrick. "It could be one of a dozen things."

"It was something they thought of up there," said the Inspector very slowly. "Something important enough to unship the frame for—and afterward they came down to the excavation."

"How d'you know they didn't take it when they went back?"

"They didn't go back," said the Inspector soberly. "They'd have taken their rucksacks if they'd gone back. They wouldn't have left them there for anybody to find in daylight. They weren't covered in any way, sergeant?"

"No, sir. Just left."

Almost to himself the Inspector murmured, "Something they planned to do then. Something"—he called up the word from innumerable police courts—"something premeditated."

"Rubbish!" barked Carrick.

Manson shook his head wearily. "You're wrong, Inspector. You're so wrong!"

The Inspector came to a sudden conclusion. "If they didn't pick up the bags, they're still on this side of the Whin Sill." He glared down into the wide valley of the Tyne, slowly becoming visible in the morning light. Pulling himself up, he strode to the squad car. "Get me the station commander at Ouston!" he ordered briskly, and waited while contact was established. "Group Captain Kenley? It's Inspector Weatherly. I was told to make contact with you directly, sir. Will you run the search along the South Tyne valley, south of the Wall? If you could work over the moorland for a start . . ." He paused for a moment and listened. "That's right, sir—three children—one of them carrying a pack of some sort." And then, as an afterthought, "If you see a car in open country pulled off the road—anything that looks suspicious—let us know as soon as you can. Is there any word on the helicopters yet? Not before eight o'clock? Well, that will have to do, won't it?"

Manson had walked over to him. "For God's sake, Weatherly, tell them the childen may be in trouble! They may be with the car. They may be held."

"I've asked them to report anything suspicious," said Weatherly coldly. "—anything."

17

They sat silent, waiting. The people from Housesteads were talking with one of the policemen. The other sat by himself in the car, waiting on the radio. The two other cars that had come up during the night had been sent off to search particular areas. Down in the valley there was a car from The Twice Brewed. Its driver sat with the people from Housesteads.

The constable in the squad car called out, and as Weatherly walked toward him, they could hear the words, "Superintendent's on his way up, sir, with the communications van." He listened for a moment and then said, "Nothing from the bridges at Crow Hall, Haydon, Bridgend, and Hexham. No reports on the car."

"Right!" said Weatherly.

Carrick got to his feet ponderously and walked over to the hut. Without going inside, he reached in and took the Primus stove from its shelf. Putting it down on the floor of the hut, he began to pump it up. He stopped abruptly and called out, "Inspector!"

The Inspector walked over.

Carrick pointed. "I think you missed that last night."

The Inspector said, "Blood, by . . . !" He crouched down.

There were three elongated spots of blood on the rough timber below the floor level and spots on the grass beneath and on a patch of hardened earth. They were quite clear now in the growing light.

Carrick said slowly and bluntly, "He was struck as he lay in his blankets on the floor. Prentice rested like that; I remember discussing it with him. Blake was there."

Manson had come over to them. "I took the blankets from the floor. He *must* have been lying in them." He went up the side of the hut, turned, and came back. "Somebody came down this side, turned the corner, and hit out. He never had a chance." He faced the Inspector challengingly. "Do you think my children would do a thing like that? A boy of fifteen, a girl of thirteen . . . ?"

Doggedly the Inspector repeated Blake's words: " 'The children tried . . .' " He paused for a second. " 'They stunned me.' "

Furiously Manson stormed at him, "There were words between! You run two things together that have no connection—no vestige of connection. He might have said, 'The children tried to help me.' Prove that he didn't! Prove that he didn't!"

Carrick put his hand on his arm. "Steady! *We* know that they couldn't have done it. The Inspector doesn't. He's got to take the evidence as he sees it. It'll clear itself."

"Evidence!" said Manson bitterly. "Words out of context from a man with a fractured skull!"

The Inspector turned away from both of them and crouched down, studying the tiny spots of blood.

Carrick reached past him, picked up the Primus, and carried it to one of the blocks that lay level on the ground. He finished pumping it up and went back to the hut for methylated spirits. He asked coolly, "Will I do any damage if I get coffee and biscuits out?"

"As long as you step over this," answered the Inspector, his voice quiet.

The Professor busied himself for a moment inside the hut. He came out carrying a kettle of water and the coffeepot. "It'll have to be black. Milk's not due yet."

Weatherly looked up at him. He said, as if he were trying to offer something, "You really *don't* believe that they could have done it, do you?" His voice was pitched low so that Manson could not hear.

"I know they didn't," stated the Professor calmly. "I know that they couldn't. It's as simple as that."

"Nothing's as simple as that"—the Inspector almost whispered the words—"nothing. We get to know that. Sometimes it frightens one. If you're right, where are they?"

The Professor opened his arms in a gesture of helplessness made almost ludicrous by the kettle and the coffeepot. "I don't know. They may have started by chasing whoever it was that attacked Blake, thinking they could handle it on their own. Blake might have meant that the children tried to stop them. After that there's nothing more than guesswork."

"If they were chasing someone, they must at least have passed a place with people by now. One of them could have broken away. One of them could have spoken to a policeman —gone and hammered on the door of a pub—anything to get help. But they haven't."

"They may have started by chasing and been chased themselves. They may be tied up somewhere in an outhouse —in a wood even."

The Inspector made no comment. Instead he said obliquely, "It's a big prize, a tremendous prize."

Carrick shuddered for an instant and went down to the Primus.

Behind him the constable said, "Sup'rintendent's comin' up, sir."

Clinton's foot slipped from the tussock, and he plunged down all the way to his knee. He grabbed at Peter, and Peter held him while he pulled clear. The green surface remained open for a minute, and below it the water was peat dark and dangerous-looking. He said, "It's a swamp."

"Peat hag. Watch your feet, Mig! The tussocks'll carry us . . ." Peter paused and added doubtfully, "I think."

Mig said revengefully, "It won't carry the big one over there!" She jerked her head to the west. They could still hear one of the men plainly, blundering along in the half-light. A hundred and fifty yards behind them there was another man running silently, menacingly. Beyond him was a third, well over to the east.

Peter grunted. "If we knew how deep it was . . ."

Clinton asked, "What's it? Kind o' quicksand?"

"Peat hag," repeated Peter. "It's treacherous—can be dangerous. I went up to my waist once. Cut out to the side when I was following Dad. He pulled me out and lammed me for being stupid."

Mig was too worried to laugh. Her eyes searched from tussock to tussock. It had been wet for the last two hundred yards—more perhaps. Now it was real bog, and as the light grew, she could see that it stretched wide on either hand. Ahead of them there was one cluster of bush—heather perhaps—not high but solid-looking; firm ground if the uncertain light was not playing tricks on them.

Peter had seen it too. "I don't think they could cross this lot, and it's worse beyond. If we can make it to that clump and it's an island, we might be safe."

"It could be the other side of the bog," said Mig, afraid even to hope.

The American boy said stoutly, "Short of an angel with wings, don't see we got an option."

Again Mig was too weary to laugh.

They picked their way on, desperately careful, trying to avoid the need to jump, knowing that they were too tired, that even fear could no longer give them wings. Once Mig went in, and the boys helped her. One leg of her shorts was soaked. Peter made three tries before he found a firm tussock in a channel of stagnant water; he stood on another tussock, bending over dangerously to help first Mig and then Clinton across.

Behind them the Captain—Clinton recognized the voice —called out twice with sharp incisive orders and was answered from either side. Curlews rose, their wings clapping, from the clump. They could see now that it was in fact heather.

Peter said, "Wouldn't be if it wasn't solid ground. That voice puts the wind up me by itself."

"It'll be all right," croaked Mig, "if it isn't the other side."

They all knew that it could be a peninsula jutting out into the bog, or that, even if it were an island, the marsh beyond it might be relatively firm, capable of bearing a heavy man. The visible water channels that remained to be crossed, however, were wider still. They came to one so wide that Peter's heart failed him. Behind them the Captain called again, moving his men with quick, practiced skill. His voice was the needed stimulant. Peter jumped despairingly, missed and was waist-deep instantly, clawing at a tussock out of reach, the soft bottom sucking and gulping at his legs. His hand grasped an old and unidentifiable branch that snapped at once. Then he got a tough root, pulled himself up a little, found another, and was suddenly out of the water, the brown of it streaming off him—weed and slime and algae covering the lower part of his body.

The island clump was very close now. He thought for the first time that he could see a way from tussock to tussock. He said, "Jump, Mig! I'll get you."

Once again the Captain called at exactly the important moment, and Mig made a leap that almost burst her heart. She fell far short, but Peter was already in the water again, one hand anchored to the friendly root, the other groping for her, and she came slowly to safety, her body sucking out of the cold water.

Clinton turned and hopped back three tussocks, turned again, ran three strides, and with an enormous jump sailed over almost dry. "You gotta have training," he commented infuriatingly.

Peter disregarded him. He led the way over the last yards. The tussocks were firmer now. He knew that they could reach the islet, and in a moment he knew that it *was* an islet—stretches of open water, stretches of deep marsh lay beyond it, running from them clear up to the boundary of the forest. From the north it was impassable. From the east and west it was alike impassable—he was sure of that. There remained only the route from the south. Could the men make the crossing? Three of them were heavy. The other, the one who had shot at Mig—they had no idea of his name —was small and light.

They collapsed on the island, were hidden at once in the heather, and lay there wheezing and panting, getting back their breath.

Clinton recovered himself first. Resting on his elbows, his eye just above the level of the heather, he looked faintly like a seal. After a little he said, "Will you take a peek at this?"

Peter raised himself. Mig disregarded him, exhausted.

Clinton said, "That's the Captain. Watch!"

The Captain had reached the edge of the first open water; now he withdrew, measuring distance. He moved forward again with a rush and launched himself in a prodigious leap. He landed precisely where he had intended, on the tussock in mid-channel that the children had used. As he landed, the tussock gave way under his weight. They heard his voice, no longer level, say hotly, "Blast!" and he staggered back, thigh deep in the clutch of the peat.

Mig jerked herself up.

Clinton said very slowly and carefully, "I *think*—we've —made it."

The car came up the slope of the hill easily and cleanly, and stopped just short of the communications truck.

Manson ran down to it. "Kit, what are you doing here? I wanted you to stay at home."

"I couldn't," said his wife. "I couldn't wait any longer. I borrowed Mike's car and came. He and Mary will wait at the house for messages. They know the police number at Hexham. There was nothing I could do there. I couldn't wait."

He said gently, "There's no news yet, but there's no need to worry either. They'll turn up—they always do."

"With the most wonderful excuses." His wife smiled as if she meant it. "Your side of the family."

The Superintendent came over and saluted Mrs. Manson. The Inspector followed, a little behind him.

The Superintendent said: "We're doing everything we can, Mrs. Manson. The first aircraft should be over in about four minutes' time. They're going to sweep the whole of the Tyne Valley. We'll have helicopters later." He paused for a moment, eyeing her, and decided that optimistic words were not enough. "We have twenty cars working in the valley, Mrs. Manson, and every policeman in the area has been alerted. We'll find them."

Mrs. Manson nodded. "Mr. Blake—how is he?"

"Not too good, I'm afraid," the Inspector answered. "The doctors say that it's a depressed fracture. He's unconscious again." He smiled at her, suddenly human. "He won't die though—it's not as bad as that."

A voice called, "Here it comes!"

The plane came roaring along the valley, low down. It was a jet trainer. As it reached them, it dipped its wings rapidly in salute and flew on past Milking Gap, past The Twice Brewed, past Haltwhistle Burn to Gilsland and the Irthing.

The Inspector said, "I would have thought a slower plane . . . sir."

The Superintendent nodded. "They'll have two Piper Cubs ready by half past seven, but they're going to sweep with two of these for the time being."

The Captain stood with his feet planted firmly apart, his hands clasped behind him. Despite the fact that he was wet to his waist, he had a parade-ground air. He was alert, dangerous. The small man came up to him reluctantly, and with some old memory driving him, stood sullenly to attention.

The Captain said, "You fired that shot!"

Dent answered, the words coming out in a rush, "They'd 'a got to the trees else, Capt'in."

"You fired it." The Captain disregarded the explanation utterly.

"Yes," and then, after only the very briefest hesitation, "sir."

"You fired it because you were late getting to the trees yourself—too late to head them off."

The little man stood wordless.

"My orders were that no firearms were to be carried."

"I jus' . . ."

"Never mind what you 'just'! You had an automatic and you shot at these children. If they get you, the charge will be attempted murder now—you know that."

"Yes—sir." Again there was the slightest hesitation.

"Give it me!"

"It's gone, Capt'in. One of them hit me with a stone, knocked me out. When I came to"—he spread out an expressive hand—"gone."

"They've got it then." The hard eyes bored into the small man's brain. "I'd leave you on the moor if I didn't think that they'd get at us through you. If this had been in Borneo, I'd have had you shot for it. Get the other two over! Signal them—no more shouting. There'll be people moving in a little." He walked disgustedly away.

Clinton murmured more to himself than to the others: "Now what?"

Peter followed the direction of his eyes. "Signaling—over toward the forest—the chap that turned us away when we tried for the tower."

Clinton nodded. "He's answering." And after a minute or two, "He's moving back."

The man Dent crossed to a rock beyond the Captain, climbed on to it to give himself a wider view, and began to search to the west. Presently he repeated the signal.

"Fourth guy!" Clinton waited and added, "He's coming back too. Think they're goin' to rush us?"

"Could be," Peter answered.

Clinton made no comment, but bending down, began to search between the heather stems for stones. Mig was asleep.

Peter looked anxious. "If the four of them came at once, we couldn't hold them. They've got the gun too."

Clinton said stoutly, "We can try. Bet that short guy's not comf't'ble yet. You hear an aircraft?"

Peter jerked back. His voice was excited. "Yes! I wasn't sure."

They listened carefully for a moment. Then Clinton shook his head. "Way over to the south. A jet—jet trainer. You got an airfield hereabouts?"

"Yes, over at Ouston."

Clinton grunted, reached out, and picked up another stone. "No need for both of us to watch. Toss you for who has the first stretch." He looked at the stone. "Heads this side, tails this."

Peter called "Heads" and won. Clinton settled himself to watch the men coming back round the edges of the marsh to rejoin the Captain.

The man Cleave asked: "Do we chuck it in then?"

"We do not," said the Captain acidly. "We'll have to lie up for a long time after this. We need the money more than ever. We haven't a chance without it."

Cleave nodded. "It had to be the girl!"

"How was I to know?" Dent's voice was aggrieved. "It was dark there close to the trees. The moon wasn't high enough. Three kids—I didn't aim. I jus' shot."

"And hit the girl!" Cleave put his head between his hands. "How d'you think that will sit with a jury?"

The voice of the Captain called them back to order. "All right—it's done now! You'll get your share when we get to Paris. After that you're on your own. You understand? Meanwhile, we've got to find out if they've got the gun."

"How we goin' to find out?"

"*He's* going to find out," replied the Captain coldly. "He's going to work his way .tussock to tussock as close to them as he can. If they've got the gun, they'll take a shot at him sooner or later."

Dent said, "My God, Capt'in!"

"You start—now!"

The other two men nodded without sympathy.

"You've drawn fire before," said Edwards. "You'll do it again an' like it!" He stood up.

Dent got reluctantly to his feet, his tongue moving over his lips. "Right!" he muttered and moved toward the water.

Clinton shook Peter. "Wake up! They've bin yakkin' for six minutes. Now one of them's headin' this way."

As they watched, Dent jumped the first stretch of the deep water, landed precariously, recovered his balance, and came on. The American boy began to heft a stone up and down. They stared intently, excitement mounting.

"How far out will you be able to reach him?"

"'Tisn't a question of how far," replied Clinton with calculation. "Some place he's goin' to slip and get into the deep water. Then he's goin' to be stuck till he clears himself—that's the time to pound him."

"Who?" Mig sat up, half awake.

"Little guy," said Clinton, without turning. "Keep your head down! He was the one had the gun."

Mig shivered.

Dent had crossed two of the channels now. There was a stretch of tussocks within easy jumping; he came upon them rapidly. They could see his face clearly in the morning light. One eye was black and swollen, and there was a cut above it across the right temple—dried blood made the wound look enormous.

Peter said, "He's not carrying the gun."

"Somethin' flew away when I rocked him—reckon that was it." Clinton stood up sharply as Dent jumped. "Won't make it," he grunted and poised himself ready to throw.

The man landed ludicrously in the water, shook himself, and lifted his head. In that moment Clinton threw. The stone took Dent on the right cheekbone just below the earlier wound. He fell face forward into the water again.

"If he drowns . . . ?" began Peter.

"Let him!" Clinton snapped with a sudden fury. "He shot Mig, didn't he?"

"He's moving." Cleave's tone was utterly callous. "Lifted his head. He's turning. That boy's lethal with a stone. Shall I go get him?"

"He can find his own way back." The Captain's voice was inhuman. "We *still* don't know if they have the automatic. We *do* know that they're dangerous with stones. You two get back to where you were. Make a float—a small raft— something that you can push in front of you on the surface —enough to cover head and shoulders against stones. When we signal you, work your way up the open water at the back of the islet. Don't try to wade! That's what they want. They're not fools, these children. They waited for Dent."

"How do we fix a raft?" asked Edwards doubtfully.

"You've got knives. There's enough wood about. Cut pine branches to size and lash them."

"With what?"

The Captain stared at him with a frosty eye. "Use your shirt sleeves! Cut them out, slit them into four. Don't you remember anything that you were taught on your survival course?"

"And you?"

"Dent and I will take them in front. They'll have to divide their fire between four targets." He paused for a moment. "There won't be enough stones on that islet."

18

Peter asked, "Where'd you learn to throw like that?"

"Baseball," said Clinton contentedly. "You'd never learn it at cricket. Meant to hit his left eye."

"Liar!" Mig remembered again the outrage in Dent's face as the stone struck. "*He* won't come back."

"The others are too heavy." Peter permitted himself a measure of optimism. "We're safe if we can stick it out."

Mig nodded. "We *can* stick it out."

Peter shook his head. "It isn't just being brave or anything like that. We're all right for water, but we haven't had anything to eat since yesterday lunch—and we're cold *and* wet."

"I'd forgotten!" Mig fished in the big pocket of her shirt. The bar of chocolate looked incomprehensibly small in the light of their need. It was misshapen, melted first by the heat in the long pursuit, part melted again by water. Divided in three, it was barely more than a mouthful apiece —but it was, at least, a mouthful.

"Can do," said Clinton, and stared at Mig for a little. "You know, you're quite a guy!"

The girl flushed with pleasure.

Peter said, disregarding the interchange, "We've got to

get dry. Take your things off, Mig!" He turned to the bulky, formless bundle in the rucksack straps. "Take 'em off and put this on! It's pretty well dry 'spite of the way I went into the water. We'll put our things on the tops of the bushes. That'll help anybody who's looking for us to see where we are. Sun'll be up in a few minutes, and they'll dry out. It's going to be cold till then."

Mig knelt over the bundle, undoing the knot that she had tied with the sleeves of the sweater; she had already loosened the straps. When the knot was undone, she lifted it clear and slowly peeled it up. The back of the dish was encrusted with lime and oxidation. Otherwise it was smooth. The low rim of the foot stood out unblemished, but two inches from it at one point there was a deep round indentation. The metal itself was pushed in in a shallow depression round it, and in the hollow of the mark it shone brilliant, clean, and—as Mig said afterwards—"silver." They stared at it soberly. Mig's face had gone a little white.

Peter said, awed, "If you hadn't been carrying it . . . !"

"And you came round and ran another mile after!" Clinton's tone was as shocked as Mig's face.

She shuddered, unable for a second to control herself. Then, with enormous care and very slowly, she turned the dish round.

The three of them gasped simultaneously. Despite the dark matt surface of the oxidation, the design stood out boldly beautiful. At each quarter of the circle was the figure of a girl—the work, beyond all question, of a great master. The grace, the life, the rhythm of the figures was incomparable.

To the left of the rounded ugliness of the bullet mark was the figure of the girl that Mig's fingers had discovered yesterday—only yesterday, she thought wonderingly. She was slender, infinitely joyous, her hands above her head, as Mig had described them, her face turned up, watching a flight of birds that seemed to spring from between her hands and swirl round the inside of the rim in a moving, delicate pattern of wings.

At the next quarter the girl was naked, her arms raised in a great V. Birds swirled past them, their wings cutting across them, so that she stood below a stream of flight with her upspread hands immersed in it.

The third figure was turned toward them, her hands held up enchantingly with food. The birds were swooping at them—land birds, some of them tiny, some of them with great sweeping wings, all of them precisely and perfectly observed. Beyond her the land birds thinned out. They were mostly gulls now, sea birds—a cormorant here and there, terns, kittiwakes.

They flew to the fourth figure. The impression that was given was that they flew faster, that the wind was rising, that the fourth figure was bowed with her back to it, her hair streamed out in its fury, her clothes billowed ahead of her, and that beyond her the gulls went on, diminished, driven before a gale until at last they were lost in it like shadows of birds seen over the sea at night.

The three were quite silent—for how long they could not afterward tell. They had forgotten their cold and hunger.

Once Mig said softly, moving her finger from figure to figure, "Spring, summer, autumn, winter."

The feet of the figures rested alternately on spray or on calm water, and beneath them a circle of dolphins, elaborately intertwined, moving as lively as real dolphins at the bow of a ship under sail, made a broad pattern of a different beauty. In the precise center of the dish, small but exquisitely modeled, were four seahorses, their tails entwined in a formal, intricate device.

It was Mig who broke the silence the second time. Very softly she whispered, "It was worth it."

Contentedly, almost in a daze, she slipped off her wet things, pulled the sweater over her head, stretched it as far down as she could for decency's sake, found a safety-pin that she always kept with providential pessimism in her shirt pocket, and pinned it together at the bottom. She picked up the transistor radio and put it squarely in the sun to dry. "Proba'ly never work again," she said resignedly as she settled herself down beside the dish.

"Probably," corrected Peter automatically, and added, apparently at cross-purposes, "Bit of water won't stop *it*."

Mig said, "I don't mind—I don't mind," and was instantly two thirds asleep, her fingers stroking and stroking the girl that she had christened Spring.

Mrs. Manson tried not to listen, but the loudspeaker was compulsive. She could hear the voices, some of them rasping, some of them oddly angry, some of them detached and all but disembodied.

"Patrol car reports spotting five childen."

Mrs. Manson had heard too many reports now to place the slightest hope on this. Village children, they would be, on their way to school across a field path.

Somebody had found an abandoned car at Haydon Bridge, but both its headlamps were intact, and somebody else remembered that it had been there for three days.

Kielder kept coming back with reports that no one had seen anything suspicious. Kielder seemed almost over-anxious to clear itself.

Hexham had discovered a mysterious van that had passed through to the Chollerford road the previous evening with somebody drunk in the back.

Every now and then, over the hum and uncertainty

of the police broadcast, came the flat metallic voices of the observers in the Piper Cubs reporting to base.

Nothing . . . nothing . . . nothing.

The Superintendent sat silent. The Inspector had long since gone off to investigate a rumor on Thorngrafton Common. With the others the Superintendent listened to the loudspeakers. At last he took his pipe out of his mouth, knocked out the dottle on the stone, and stood up. For a long minute he watched the Piper Cubs quartering backwards and forwards above Thorngrafton. To the watchers on the hill it was clear that they had found nothing significant, that they were watching and hoping—and that was all.

The Superintendent said, "Time we moved over the hill." He called the sergeant to him and began to discuss the availability of patrol cars. "Farm to farm," he said at length. "A car up here, a car on the Simonburn road, a car up the Greenhaugh road. Stop at every farmhouse, ask every shepherd, every man they see in a field. Car up the Stell Green track, car over at Hotbank, two cars over the Peel road. Every farm—and I mean every farm. Usual questions: see anything yesterday evening, hear anything in the night, dogs barking? They're countrymen; they don't miss much. Tell the operations room I want it done, and I want it done quickly! Report back the smallest thing!"

He looked down the slope. "Who's this now?"

The Professor followed his glance. "My people." Automatically he looked at his watch. "Miss Kirton—on time as usual—Prentice." Another car turned in at the gate from the road. "This'll be Witton."

"Want to question 'em," said the Superintendent briefly.

The little knot of people seemed to come up the slope of the hill almost reluctantly. Miss Kirton was in the lead as they approached the main group. She looked from side to side absolutely bewildered; but when she came to Carrick where he stood next to the Superintendent, it was clear that she had arrived at an explanation.

She said simply, "*Not* the dish?"

Carrick began to speak. Easily the Superintendent said, "Just a minute, sir, if you don't mind. I'd like to talk to each of you separately. You first, please, Miss . . . ?" His voice rose in a question.

"Miss Kirton."

He took her over to the patrol car, opened the rear door, and ushered her in. To a constable sitting in the front passenger seat he said, "Take a note, please, Reardon!"

"What time did you leave yesterday evening, Miss Kirton?"

Step by step he ran over her memory of the previous day. When her description reached the road on the way home, he stopped and went back. "And the three children were . . . ?"

"Talking to Mr. Blake," said Miss Kirton promptly. "I know—I turned back as we reached the road."

"Why?"

"I don't know—I just did."

"Who else was there?"

"Mr. Witton."

"Good. Now I am going to ask you one more question— a matter of opinion, not of fact. Do you think that those three children would have taken the dish?"

"Of course not!" Miss Kirton allowed herself to snap at the Superintendent. "What a ridiculous idea!"

The Superintendent watched her carefully. "They've disappeared," he said abruptly.

"No, oh, no! Oh, poor Mig! What d'you mean, disappeared?"

"Mr. Blake," replied the Superintendent evenly, "was attacked. He has a fractured skull. The dish was stolen. The children failed to telephone at eight o'clock, as they had promised, from The Twice Brewed, and there has been no vestige of a sign of them since."

Miss Kirton turned and stared at the Superintendent. Her face was coldly angry, but instead of defending them, she attacked. "And you've not found them? With all this—with the airplanes too—you haven't found that child?" She paused for a moment, remembering Mig's face as she traced the figure the previous afternoon. "Are you proud of yourself?"

The Superintendent nodded very slowly. "No," he answered, "I'm not."

Quietly, methodically, the interrogation went on. One after the other the members of the team told their stories and gave their views. Not one of them would admit the slightest possibility of the children's having taken the dish, not one of them until it came to Witton's turn. He answered the Superintendent's questions reluctantly.

"You stayed on after the others. Why?"

"I had things to do."

"Do you often stay after the others?"

"We mostly go together," replied Witton morosely. "Have a drink on the way home."

"But you didn't yesterday?"

"I'd left my car over at Millking Gap."

"Why?"

"Wanted to walk along the Wall before I started work."

"Do you often do that?"

"First time. There's no rule against it."

"Did anyone know you were going to do that?"

"Everybody," answered Witton, a shade too hastily. "I'd talked about it the night before."

The Superintendent fired his question about the children brusquely.

For the first time Witton hesitated. Finally he answered, "I don't know."

The Superintendent's face showed no particular flicker of interest. "You think they might have?"

"I don't know."

The Superintendent altered the question very slightly. "You think they could have?"

"Yes." Witton spoke this time without any hesitation at all. "They could have."

"Did they strike you as balanced, sensible children?"

"Uppish," answered Witton, once again a thought too quickly.

"You don't like children, Mr. Witton?"

"Not on a dig," said Witton crustily. "They're a nuisance. They get in the way; they're cheeky."

"Could they physically have shifted the blocks of stone?"

"With a crowbar, yes. Sheer vandalism!"

"Would they have known how to?"

"That boy would."

The Superintendent turned on him fully. "Could they have given Blake a fractured skull?"

"You never know with children these days."

"Meaning . . . ?"

"Mods, Rockers, pep pills, violence . . ."

"*These* children?"

"Why, the girl went off listening to a pop group with a transistor set in the middle of the work . . ."

"Thank you, Mr. Witton," said the Superintendent. Through the open car window he watched him speculatively as he walked away.

Mig yawned, turned over flat on her back, winced, and opened her eyes. She felt much too lazy to sit up.

Peter said, "All right! You can dress now. Your things are dry. You're hardly half decent."

Mig smiled happily at him. "I've got the dish! I—just—don't—care. When are we going to be rescued?"

Clinton, sitting up a couple of yards away, said, "The Captain's still there, and there's no sign of the cops. *We'd* have had sirens all across the hills by now."

"All you get for it is bigger and better murders," said Peter defensively.

"Not doing so good yourselves these days," retorted Clinton.

They felt ridiculously lighthearted in reaction to the night's terror. They were almost sure that the four could not get at them, sure that they no longer had a revolver, sure that it would be possible to outlast them.

Mig finished changing and settled herself propped on her elbows, with her face above the dish. The figure of Spring was bright now from the gentle polishing of her fingers.

Peter, watching her trace its outline, said, "You were doing that all the time you were asleep."

"I know. I dreamed about it. It's the most beautiful thing I've ever seen."

"Or any of us." The American boy's voice, almost for the first time, was completely without double meaning.

Peter sat with his arms round his knees. "They're bound to begin to search up here in an hour or two. I expect they've been searching all around the Wall first. I've been thinking. If they"—he jerked his thumb over to where the Captain and Dent were partly hidden between stunted bushes—"if they try to get at us again, I'm going to tell them that if they come closer we'll sink it in the deep water."

Mig clutched at the dish fiercely. "You couldn't!"

He nodded soberly. "I could. Frogmen would get it out

in a few hours at the most, but *they* couldn't. If they know that, they might pack it up."

Mig said, "If only we could see somebody—shout at somebody!"

"We're about in the worst place on the moor for that." Peter nodded, for the first time allowing a shadow of doubt to creep into his voice.

"What about one of those shepherd guys?"

"Last place you'd see one," answered Peter. "They'd never allow sheep to come within a quarter of a mile of this bog."

"Forestry guys?"

"With the water and sweat and one thing and another I can't read the map, but I think that this bog is the head of the Saughy Sike. Not even a track anywhere near it."

"The how much?"

"Saughy Sike. Your father would have to let you stay on in England for a year at least to learn the language," said Peter mockingly.

Clinton rolled over on his back, chewing a straw. "And she had the nerve to nag about Tallahassee and Kankakee!"

"That was years ago," said Mig fondly, working at a little piece of dirt between the wings of a jay with her fingernail. "Every feather—every feather. What's the time?"

"My watch's stopped," Peter complained. "I'd say it was round about eleven."

Clinton held up his wrist. "Waterproof," he said belligerently, "shockproof, antimagnetic. It's quarter of eleven."

"Doesn't matter." Mig almost sang, her heart was so full. "Doesn't matter as long as it's not quarter past twelve."

"Why?"

"The Mosspickers!"

"After last night?" Peter's voice was totally puzzled. "What difference does last night make?"

Clinton grinned provocatively at her. "Bet it's made a difference to your transistor set anyways!"

Peter picked up the set. It was quite dry, and he switched it on. For a long half minute he worked the little milled wheel with his thumb. There was no response whatever. "No Mosspickers," he said with finality. "No moss."

19

The Superintendent lumbered over to where Manson sat with his wife. They were quite silent, tense, waiting. As he approached, Manson said heavily, "Well?"

"One of the hands at Hotbank Farm saw the lights of a car down in the valley."

"Two lights or one?"

"He didn't notice," replied the Superintendent slowly. "He wasn't interested. Could have been somebody going up to . . ." He paused. "Bonnyrigg Hall, is it?"

Manson picked up the map that he had been poring over. "Yes, it would be."

"The helicopters will be here in half an hour," said the Superintendent, as if he were offering comfort.

Manson grunted.

"There's an American plane coming."

Manson looked up sharply. "Clint's father?"

The Superintendent turned to him inquiringly.

"He's in the Embassy, but he has something to do with the American Air Force bases. He could get an aircraft."

"Would it be another jet?"

"I expect so," said Manson, dismissing it automatically as useless.

"This boy Clinton"—the Superintendent went on to the question with perfect naturalness—"what sort of a boy is he? I don't know about American children. Would he be a Mod or a Rocker?"

Mrs. Manson half turned and stared at him.

"Neither," said Manson, his voice sharper still. "He's a normal, reasonable boy."

"And yours?"

Mrs. Manson broke in before her husband could answer. "Neither Mod nor Rocker," she said firmly. "Ordinary children, ordinarily intelligent."

"Mad on pop music?"

"Not mad." Mrs. Manson's voice sharpened in turn like her husband's. "Mig has crazes. She's wildly keen on some group called the Mosspickers now."

"Keen enough to carry a transistor radio to listen in to them?"

Manson sat up abruptly, but he did not speak.

His wife said, "Who told you about that?"

"Mr. Witton," answered the Superintendent evenly. "I don't think he likes children"—he paused for a moment— "or pop music."

Mrs. Manson frowned.

"There wasn't a transistor set in the rucksacks," said the Superintendent.

Manson jerked up his hand in sudden decision. "Super-intendent, can I have a police car?"

"Why?"

Manson looked at his watch. "If Mig is . . ." He hesitated imperceptibly, refusing to consider the use of the word "alive." "If Mig's hands are free, she'll tune in to the Moss-pickers at twelve o'clock. If I can use a police car, I can get to the studio in Newcastle by twelve. They can interrupt the broadcast for a police message. We can tell the children to make some signal—to give us some sign to show where they are. Make a fire if they're in the open—make smoke —smash a window if they're in a house—shout—scream— anything! I'll tell them that the aircraft are overhead searching. They'll find some way—after all there are three of them! One of them must be able to give us some clue as to where they are."

The Superintendent turned away. He did not even bother to answer Manson. He called, "Sergeant! Take Mr. Manson in your car. Thirty miles . . . you've thirty-three minutes to make it—and you'll lose a couple of minutes before you get to the road. We'll have two motorcyclists at Throckley crossroads to help you in through the city."

Mrs. Manson had risen. She was suddenly quivering with excitement. "Hurry!" she urged her husband. "Oh, hurry!"

Manson raced down the slope to the car. In a minute it was lurching and bounding its way down to the valley bottom.

Peter said, "That's the third time I've seen that plane."

Clinton followed it with his eyes. "Piper Cub or somethin'. If he comes a bit closer, maybe we could signal to him."

"How?" asked Peter flatly.

"Dunno. If we had a mirror, maybe we could flash a mirror."

"If we had a phone, maybe we could phone."

Mig said, "Keep your shirt on!"

Peter disregarded her. Worriedly he began, "If they can hold us here till tonight . . ."

Mig was still studying the dish. "Won't be dark till nine o'clock. That's another nine hours."

"Nine and a quarter," said Clinton pedantically, looking at his watch. "It's a quarter of twelve."

Automatically Mig reached over, picked up the transistor set and moved the wheel. Once again there was no result. "Absolutely dead," she said, mourning.

Lazily Clinton ordered, "Hand it over! If Peter'll lend me a knife, I'll see what I can do."

"Oh, please!" begged Mig. "Please!"

Clinton put the transistor set on the turf beside him and studied it. Abstractedly he began to scrape beneath his fingernails with the point of the blade. "Where'd you get this thing?" he asked loftily.

"It's not a thing! It's *my* transistor!" retorted Mig positively. "Do something to it!"

Tentatively the boy began to strain at the screw on the back of the set. It gave after a moment or two, and he loosened it carefully.

As he shifted it, Peter exclaimed, "They're on the move!"

Hastily Clinton put down the transistor. "Signalin' again!"

They watched the small man semaphoring rapidly, and half turning, saw the answer from the edge of the forest. The signal was repeated to the westward, and they saw the answer from the fourth man.

Clinton said, "I reckon it's about time you told them that you're goin' to sink the dish."

Mig whispered, heartbroken, "Not yet! Oh, not yet!"

They saw the small man turn, as if for instructions, to the Captain, and then turning again, head toward them. Behind him the Captain moved purposefully to the edge of the bog.

Peter stood up, cupped his hands round his mouth and called. He had proposed to shout "Ahoy!" but it seemed ridiculous here in the center of England. The sound came out as a strangled "Oi!" It was, none the less, enough. Both men stopped. Peter shouted slowly and distinctly, "If you try . . . anything . . . we're going to throw the dish . . . into . . . deep . . . water!"

The Captain's voice was hard and unimpressed. It carried back utterly clearly without aid from his hands. "If you try anything as stupid as that, you force me to use this." He held up a black object, square and ugly.

"Gun," said Clinton unhappily.

"One of you will get badly hurt this time!"

"It's a long shot." Clinton was trying to judge the possibilities.

"Bring the dish out, and we'll let you go clear. You have my word that you won't be hurt."

Mig said, "When a beast like that begins to talk about his 'word' . . ."

"Are you sure it *is* a gun?" demanded Peter.

"No." Clinton's voice was still unhappy. "But I'm not sure it's not!"

"What do we do?"

"Wait," said Mig urgently, "wait! They'll have to get a lot closer before they can do anything. We can tell if it's a gun then. What are the other two doing?"

"I'd forgotten them!" Peter was desperately worried. "They're working away at something bulky on the water —something that floats."

Clinton watched intently for a moment. "Cover against stones," he guessed. "We're goin' to want a lotta ammunition. We need a stockpile."

The car had reached the top of the long slope down to Newcastle. The road stretched before them straight and wide, the ancient road that was built on the top of the Wall —the Military Road. The strap pulled at Manson's chest as the driver swung out to pass traffic. The motorcyclists ahead swept oncoming vehicles out of their way and held the crossing traffic against the lights. He had never been driven like this before, nor perhaps would he ever be driven so again. They had six minutes to go—six minutes of the crowded city traffic. The car slowed violently, shot ahead again, found a gap, and moved through another potential block.

Manson said, "The Super will have told the broadcasting people?"

"Done it through the information room," replied the sergeant confidently.

"He's not as slow as he looks . . ." began Manson.

"He's not slow." The sergeant's mouth shut down like a trap. Then, relaxing, "Had him after me once." And after another pause, reminiscently, "Not slow."

"Are we going to do it?"

" 'Course we're goin' to do it!"

Manson saw a clock—three minutes to twelve. But street clocks were always unreliable. They skimmed between two buses, and he was quite certain that there was a clearance of barely an inch on either side. For the first time they were halted at a solid block, the motorcyclists penned just ahead of them; then the block cleared magically, and they were through, and instantly caught in another and through that too. And then he was plunging through a sudden-forming crowd with the motorcyclists ahead of him, and somebody was saying, "First floor! Quicker by the stairs. . . ."

"Fewer than I thought." Clinton contemplated the second of the two heaps that constituted their stockpile of ammunition. The black earth had yielded singularly few good throwing stones. He had placed the piles strategically towards the ends of the islet. As he scrabbled in the water for the last visible pebble, he saw the transistor out of the corner of his eye. With a wry humor he picked it up between finger and thumb.

"Keep this for the last," he said, grinning sympathetically at Mig. "Hit him in the right place, it'd knock the brains out of anybody, if he had a brain."

Mig's eyes were very close to tears. It was too much now —too much after the night and the revolver shot, the cold and the wet and the hunger.

He said gently, "Cheer up! They won't get it," and idly fiddled with the wheel of the transistor.

Thin, reedy, disembodied, a voice said: "You have been listening to Mrs. Emmanual Ferguson. . . ."

Mig held out her hands, disregarding the valediction. She wanted to say something ridiculous and brave, and all she could say was, "Ple-e-ase!" Her thumb slipped on the little milled wheel, found it again, and the familiar raucous avalanche of the Mosspickers' signature tune blared out over the stillness. Mig plumped down on the grass beside the dish. One hand found its way automatically to the figure of Spring, the other held tightly to the transistor set. There was a brief pause. She waited for the first song. The silence grew. There seemed to be voices whispering in the background, and then suddenly, rasping and metallic, she heard a voice, "This is a police announcement . . ." And then, incredibly, impossibly, her father's voice.

"Mig—Mig Manson—if you can hear this, listen carefully. We think you are being held by somebody. We are searching for you. We have aircraft and helicopters hunting. We have police cars everywhere. Do something to help us. If you are in a house, smash the windows—throw something out. If you're in the open, set fire to the grass, the bushes. Even if you're in the forest, set fire to something. Make smoke if you can—make it as quickly as you can—make as much as you can!"

The first voice took over. "This is an urgent police message," it repeated. "Anyone seeing smoke or hearing anything unusual in the area north and south of the Roman Wall between the North Tyne and the Irthing please report immediately to your nearest police station."

Again there was a pause. A third voice said, with a slightly surprised cheerfulness, "All right, folks!" And the Moss-pickers swept into their opening song with a heavy beat on the drums.

Peter cried, "Dad! That was Dad! He said 'Make smoke!'"

Mig was crying now in earnest, cheerful, excited, happy tears, and scrabbling round for dry stuff with an immediate practicality.

Clinton wet his finger and held it up. "Any wind there is, is from there." He pointed to the south. "Will this heather stuff burn?"

"If you can get it started properly," answered Peter. "Got any paper?"

Clinton dived for the scraps of Mig's chocolate paper. She had tucked it tidily under a heather stem. They grabbed handfuls of grass, dried leaves, broken twigs—anything they could find. There was precious little of it. Peter piled it in the middle of the densest clump of heather. That would be dry now, he thought, after the long morning.

Mig, reaching down for burnable rubbish at the very edge of the water, looked up, and saw the Captain heading through the shallows. She yelled, "Quick! He's coming!" and when Peter asked, "Who?" she said, "The Captain," and turned away to look over to the forest edge.

Something was moving in the water. She could see splashing and an irregular shape of timber and a man's head and arms resting on it. "And the third man . . ." she added.

Peter did not even bother to look up.

Clinton said, squinting quickly from one point to the other, "Okay! We got time."

Peter was feeling in his pockets one after the other. He found the cigarette lighter in the third, pulled it out, opened it hurriedly, and pressed it. It clicked. Nothing happened. He clicked it again—again—again. "Wet!" he said despairingly. "I never thought . . ."

Clinton stretched out his hand. "Gimme!" For a moment he held the lighter, separating the threads of the wick. Then he turned it upside down and shook it. Finally he turned it up again and pressed it. Then he looked up and grinned engagingly at Peter. "Cheap Japanese!" he said mockingly. A clear flame shot up. "Next time buy American."

"Thank God!" said Peter fervently, and made a prayer of it.

The paper lit instantly, and the grass above it. For a long doubtful minute the heather resisted, and then as a sudden, unexpected puff of wind caught it, crackled and began to burn. Before that, there had been no smoke. Now suddenly it swelled up. They pulled heather bushes and flung them on the fire. It became a sort of mad race. They were all of them wildly excited, at the edge of losing control of themselves. The fire began to move downwind, passing from one bush to another.

The Captain was shouting at them, his voice for the first time uncontrolled, but they could barely hear his words over the crackle of the flame. The other man was shouting too, but they could no longer see him for the smoke.

Clinton threw a last bush to the flames and turned, saying, "Time to deal with you, buddy-buddy!" and picked up four stones. With an almost incredible speed he threw them one after another. The fourth hit.

The Captain stumbled. Even as Clinton began a jubilant shout, he recovered himself and came steadily on again.

The other man jerked back his arm and a stone whistled past Peter's head.

Clinton ducked and said exultantly, "Wasn't a gun then! They wouldn't be throwin' stones else." With something like triumph he stooped to pick up another handful.

In that moment Peter shouted, "The fourth man!"

20

A fresh voice rasped out from one of the loudspeakers of the communications van. It had an explosive quick-fire delivery. It said, "I see smoke! Patch of moorland running into the forest—four–five miles north of the Wall." It was American.

Instantly an English voice crossed it. "Smoke rising!" Then carefully and crisply it gave map coordinates.

The American voice said again, "There's a patch of forest no'th of the lakes. It's no'thwest of that."

Again the crisp English voice came in, one of the voices from the Piper Cubs that they were already accustomed to. "It's on Henshaw Common, just beyond the line of the crags."

Again the American voice cut across. "In a swamp—islet in a swamp."

Another voice came in. "Red Searcher to Blue Searcher: Tallyho! Tallyho! Follow me! Keep down to the tree level!"

A man on the ground next to the set said, "The helicopters!"

Another loudspeaker on the police net announced apologetically, "Kielder has nothing to report. Tyne bridges, roadblocks—nothing to report."

Then, superimposed on the last words: "Bell Crags fire

tower: smoke bearing two-eight-three degrees—distant one mile and three quarters."

Again the helicopter voice. "Going in. I can see the fire." And then, "Red Searcher: I'll take the kids. Look for any men around!"

The police-net speaker said, "Patrol car X213 reports blue Zephyr, one head lamp missing, hidden in plantation Bonnyrigg track."

Nobody paid the slightest attention. Their ears were tuned compulsively to the Air Force wavelengths.

They heard the helicopter voice again. "Red Searcher to base: Three bods on islet in peat bog. Fire burning."

The Professor put his arm tenderly over Mrs. Manson's shoulders. "Kit, Kit," he said, as he felt the shudders running through her, "he said bods—not bodies. They couldn't have started a fire if they hadn't been alive. It's all right. I tell you! They're in time. It's all right!"

And then the helicopter voice again. "Red Searcher to Blue: Get that bastard! End of the islet. Get him quick! You can make it with an abseil!"

The Superintendent, his ear cocked towards the loudspeakers, saw a figure moving down the hill. Hardly lifting his voice, he said, "Mr. Witton, are you going somewhere?"

Witton answered, his tone uncertain, "I'm going to have a drink. There's no possibility of work here."

"I wouldn't, Mr. Witton," said the Superintendent softly. "I think I wouldn't." He watched him, his eye speculative again, as Witton turned and came reluctantly back.

The roar of the aircraft covered the noise of the helicopters. The jet swept past at five hundred feet, screaming.

Clinton caught it for an instant in his eye and cried, "Air Force!" And, as Peter began, "Of course it's Air Force . . ." shouted him down with, "U.S. Air Force! My pop for a buck!"

Even as he made his point, everything was blotted out in the thresh and thunder of the helicopters. A thin nylon line snaked out just to windward of the islet. They looked over the heather. The fourth man had come in from the westward, cleverly using the sparse cover of the tussocks. His shield raft had grounded ten yards from the islet. He was lifting himself from the water for the final dash. Deliberately Clinton climbed to his feet, abandoning the thin shelter of the heather, ignoring the stones that came intermittently from the other two men. Carefully he judged the distance, balanced his last stone in his hand, and threw. As the fourth man jumped, the stone hit him in the stomach—he doubled up and crumpled into the water. And from the sky, sliding down the nylon line at an incredible speed in the fantastic descent of an abseil, came a man in the fighting uniform of the Royal Marines. Immediately above the figure in the water he checked, as if he had put on air brakes; then, calmly and judiciously, he jumped square on Cleave's shoulders.

Blue Searcher lifted away as he released himself from the line and left him to it. He did *not* appear to require help.

At once Red Searcher centered itself over the islet, just clear of the fire, and dropped swiftly down. The smoke began to swirl in a ring round the children. Spray mingled with it. Noise capped it. And down through the gyrating fury came a huge, solid, friendly figure.

They were all on their feet now. The winchman released himself and turned to Mig. "Come on, Number One! Up you go!"

She stooped and lifted the dish.

"I'll bring that," he said.

"Oh, no! Oh, no!" She stooped again to the transistor set.

Peter took it from her. "I'll look after it." He watched while the winchman clipped the strap round her and pulled down the toggle.

"It's quite safe," the big man said comfortingly. "Up you go!" and signaled with his arm to the aircraft above him.

The wire tightened, and Mig went up, drawing clear of the swelling smoke, the great dish clasped in her arms. From the cabin of the helicopter, hands stretched out and pulled her in. She felt her feet on the firm, vibrating floor. Suddenly, and for the first time, her knees gave way altogether under her, and she would have fallen but for an arm about her waist. She was steered to a seat and strapped in as the wire went down again.

Clinton came up next, was brought inboard, and freed himself almost professionally. "Okay!" he said. "Okay! Okay!" his voice bubbling with the release from strain.

Before he was steered to a seat, he turned and glanced down through the wide-open door. "Look! Look!" he shouted.

Mig was just able to see beyond them the second helicopter, a man at the end of its wire swinging contentedly while the chopper pursued the Captain, desperate at last, back through the shallows towards the dry.

Peter came up. They put him at the other side of Mig, and he sat quietly, smiling a little, the enormous weight of his responsibility eased now.

The winchman came up last. Even as he started up, the helicopter rose high above the smoke, high above the forest. They could see, as she turned, two police cars bucketing up over the moor and at the edge of the pines a Forestry Land-Rover. They could see the fire tower, the tongue of trees that led to Greenlee Wood where they had dodged the watchers, and the great oblong of Greenlee Wood itself. They could see over it to the loughs and then beyond them, across the valley, the line of the Wall, its north face dark in the shadow of the noonday sun, stretching for mile after mile from Sewingshields Crags to the east, in great swags across the moor to Housesteads and then, splendid and belligerent, up and down the crags to the Nine Nicks of Thirlwall.

The helicopter turned in a wide, easy curve. They heard a voice above the roar of the engine and the thresh of the rotors, and they saw the other helicopter move, fast as a dragonfly, to the edge of the forest. A man was running on the track.

Clinton's hand pinched Mig's knee. "The little guy!" he shouted.

One of the crew men came aft and bent close to them and asked, "How many were there?"

Peter held up four fingers. "Four."

The aircraftman held up three fingers in return. "Three so far."

Peter shouted back, "Fourth one under the smoke, I think —in the water."

"Good man!" The aircraftsman patted his shoulder and went for'ard to the pilot.

They circled round and round. The Captain had disappeared—into the other helicopter, they guessed. They saw for a brief second the small man being drawn up. Blue Searcher swooped back to the island. It was like a seabird over a shoal of fish, Mig thought, hovering, flighting, diving. It went down to the right of the smoke, and the rush of its wind blew the gray-white pall away. They saw the last of the gang in the water, still in the V-shaped contraption that he had fitted together. He had raised one disconsolate arm and was waving it in surrender.

"Get him!" ordered Red Searcher tersely, and turned towards the Wall.

From the loudspeaker the crisp voice came cheerfully, in answer apparently to a question that they had not heard.

"Oh, they're all right! They're tough. Undamaged, all three of 'em." Again they did not hear the question, but the voice said, "Yes, the girl had something in her arms."

Mrs. Manson turned to Carrick and let her shoulders droop in a last sign of relief.

The Superintendent said, "We'll see them in a minute."

Over his words they heard the throb of Red Searcher. As they tuned themselves to it, the throb grew to a roar, and they saw the shining swirl of the rotor blades over the skyline of the Wall. It circled over the valley and came back to them. The police had laid out a circle of white paper held down by stones on a level patch beyond the hut. Red Searcher came down tentatively, suspiciously almost. Then the winchman jumped from the open door and held up his arms. Running towards it, they saw Mig lifted from the aircraft, still clasping in her arms the great silver dish.

The roar of the engine died, the threshing of the great rotor blades fell to a whisper. Mig stood hesitant, her eyes searching the crowd of police, the people of Carrick's team, the people from Housesteads, the knot of reporters and cameramen from fifty miles around. Then her heart missed a beat as she saw her mother, and she began to run, the leaden tiredness of her legs, the ache in her back, the desperate, utter exhaustion all forgotten.

She had meant to make some dramatic gesture on landing. She had rehearsed a speech; she was going to hand back the dish nobly and with an air of sacrifice; but now she held it blindly toward the Professor's outstretched hands and flung herself at her mother. "I was so frightened," she wailed, "so tired . . . and I'm so *hun*gry!"

As swiftly as it had risen, the tension broke. Between tears and laughter the crowd closed in on them, the cameras clicking and whirring, the reporters firing questions.

The Superintendent put an end to it. In a quiet, authoritative voice he said, "All right, break it up now!" And then, as the crowd opened away from him, he asked gravely, "What happened?"

Peter nodded. "They coshed Mr. Blake," he said clearly and simply. "We were trying to warn him, but they got there first. He told us to follow them—to get the car's number."

"Did you?"

"578 FMH," said Peter automatically. "They were trying to put the dish into the trunk. They couldn't find the keys, and Mig crept in and snatched it—I'd told her to stay behind, but she didn't—and we ran, and Clint drew them off in the opposite direction and . . ." He stopped abruptly, staring at Mig in horror. She had slumped in her mother's arms, her knees wholly out of control now. As she collapsed, her shirt had pulled up. On the white skin of her back was a gigantic bruise the size of a soup plate, deep purple in the center, blue, green, and yellow towards the edges.

The police surgeon standing beside the Superintendent jumped forward and held her. His voice like iron, he asked, "What did they do that with?"

Clinton put his hands in his pockets and said, without expression, "They shot her. Automatic, point four-five, I'd guess."

There was a moment of absolute silence in the crowd, a moment of shock; then it was overlaid with a furious mixture of anger and sympathy and indignation.

The Superintendent lifted his hand. "Quiet, please! And then?" His face was set and grim.

"We picked her up," said Peter.

"And she ran—with that. She's got more guts than both of us." Clinton nodded gravely.

The police surgeon said, "You need something to pick

you up, young lady." His hands were working delicately over the area of the bruise—the skin was not broken anywhere. "Sal volatile or brandy."

"Brandy!" said Mig with a limp defiance.

And again there was laughter.

The police surgeon straightened himself while a constable went for his bag. "I still don't understand it. . . ." He frowned slightly.

"She had the silver dish on her back," explained Clinton, suddenly beginning to be tired himself, "and they hit that. You'll find the dent it made. . . ."

Wordlessly Professor Carrick held out the dish, bottom upwards. The deep hole of the bullet mark was clear for everybody to see.

"And then?"

"We ran and ran," said Mig wearily. "I don't know how long—I don't know. And then Peter found the island in the peat bog. . . ."

The roar as Blue Searcher skimmed over the Wall drowned the rest of her words. The helicopter came in, purposeful, businesslike, and dropped clear of the scattered paper circle to the left of its leader.

The winchman jumped out first. The police closed in. One by one, wet, bedraggled, and bruised, the four were pushed without ceremony to the grass. The small man—Dent—had his wrists bound together with a length of nylon cord. Three of them huddled together, the fourth stood apart, aloof, arrogant.

Clinton, close to the Superintendent, said, "That's the Captain."

The Superintendent turned to him instantly. "The *Captain*? Captain Wirrall?"

"Dunno. They just called him the Captain."

"It'll be Wirrall." There was an immense satisfaction in the Superintendent's voice.

Behind him the sergeant said, "Wanted for the Hillshead vase job an' for the Ainforth jewels—an' for another antiques job—can't remember for the minute."

"And for a string of others," the Superintendent added with finality. "Recognize the other three?"

"Cleave—the tall one. Come out o' the Army, did three little jobs and one with vi'lence. Quiet since then."

The Superintendent nodded. "And these three children . . ." A note of wonder crept into his voice.

The four men were brought into line in front of him. He stared levelly at the Captain. "Proud of yourself?" he demanded, and then forcefully, "Who fired the shot?"

There was absolute silence.

"At a child," said the Superintendent, "a young girl. All right, let's have it! Who used the gun?"

There was a long-drawn silence this time while the crowd waited, wholly still.

Clinton broke it. "The little guy." He glared triumphantly at Dent. "I marked him—the cut over his right eye. The other was later."

The Superintendent eyed the small man contemptuously and wheeled suddenly on the Captain. "But you were the leader, Wirrall—Captain Wirrall—'The Captain'! You ran your gang like a Commando unit. You're an ex-officer. You got fools to follow you because of it, but you won't do that again. People will remember that you were run ragged by three children and ended up in a peat bog." Suddenly he pounced. "Who gave you the information about the dish?"

This time the silence was longer, more portentous. Patiently the Superintendent waited.

Dent lifted his head, his bruised and battered face frightened and working beyond control. "It was . . ."

Cleave, standing beside him, kicked at his shins savagely.

"Stop that!" ordered the Superintendent evenly. "Somebody'd better talk before he does."

Again the silence fell.

It was Mig's voice which broke it, quiet and clear. "It was Mr. Witton. We saw him with them in their hideout up on the hill. He was pointing to the dig—explaining everything to them."

"It was 'im all right," said Dent, staring vindictively at Cleave.

The sergeant took Witton by the arm and pushed him forward. The man's face was like white ash, his mouth loose and apprehensive. "It's a damned lie . . ." he began, but even the bluster was hollow now.

The Superintendent looked at him with distaste. "I had them run a check on you this morning," he said heavily. "You were the only man at all the digs where things were stolen. You'll have to explain those too." His forehead was somber as he turned towards the four again. "The charges will be conspiracy, theft, assault, and grievous bodily harm—and attempted murder! Take them away!"

A small cloud, brilliant at the edges, had overrun the sun. The moment was as somber as the charge. There was a deep uneasy silence as the men were thrust towards the police cars.

The car from Newcastle came up through the wry procession at a furious speed. Manson leaped out and ran toward his wife and the children. Mig held out her arms to him. "Thank God, you're safe! We were able to pick up some of the helicopter's talk. We knew it was going to be all right."

"We saved it!" said Mig, and crumpled again onto the turf.

Carrick seized the moment. He walked swiftly to a pile of ashlar above the crowd. Standing on it, he swung the great dish above his head. Afterward Miss Kirton said that with his white hair and his sunburned face he looked like an Old Testament prophet. At the instant that he steadied its weight above him, the sun drew clear and the figure of Spring, polished in search of hope by Mig's frightened fingers, shone suddenly brilliant like a statue carved of light.

Carrick's voice was rich as a famous singer's as he said, "This is what they saved—a piece of man's work that is wholly perfect—that is one of the triumphs of art. Look at it for yourselves! Because of them it will be for all time one of the treasures of Britain." Still holding the great silver disk to the sunlight, he turned to Mig and said tenderly, "You will be remembered."

About the Author

David Divine, who is Defence Correspondent for the London *Sunday Times*, has made military studies of the Roman army and Roman fortifications in Britain, Europe, and North Africa. THE STOLEN SEASONS is the result of close research he did over the ground near Hadrian's Wall.

Mr. Divine was born in Cape Town, South Africa, and has traveled to almost every corner of the world. He has been a journalist and a war correspondent, and was awarded the Distinguished Service Medal for services with the small boats in the Dunkirk evacuation of 1940.

He is the author of numerous books of fiction and nonfiction for adults and children, many of which have been published in the United States.

Mr. Divine now lives with his family in London, England.